FORTHCOMING BOOKS BY FELICIA DONOVAN

Spun Tales coming July 2008

The
BLACK
WIDOW
agency

felicia donovan

North Las Vegas Library District
2300 Civic Center Drive
North Las Vegas, NV 89030

MIDNIGHT INK
WOODBURY, MINNESOTA

FIRST EDITION
First Printing, 2007

Book design by Rebecca Zins
Book format by Donna Burch
Cover design by Ellen Dahl
Cover art © InspireStock/PunchStock
Editing by Connie Hill

Midnight Ink, an imprint of Llewellyn Publications

Library of Congress Cataloging-in-Publication Data for *The Black Widow Agency* is on file at the Library of Congress
ISBN: 978-0-7387-1082-2

Midnight Ink
Llewellyn Publications
2143 Wooddale Drive, Dept. 978-0-7387-1082-2
Woodbury, MN USA 55125-2989

www.midnightinkbooks.com

Printed in the United States of America

ACKNOWLEDGMENTS

To the best literary agent, Jill Grosjean, who took a chance and made this all happen.

To the folks at Midnight Ink Books who pulled this all together, especially editor Barbara Moore.

To my first readers and gal pals, Joan Scagliotti, Marlo Ryan, Nackey Scagliotti, Denise Boyea, Tere Bowen-Irish, and Kristyn Rogers-Bernier (who planted the seed for *The Black Widow Agency* in my head). Much love and thanks to all of you for always being there for me.

To Doreen "Ethel" Gulley—the best pal I've never met, love "Lucy."

To my parents and siblings for their unwavering love and support always.

Finally, to my children, Jess and John, with all my love for all you are. Don't ever forget to dream…

Hell hath no fury like a woman scorned.

—WILLIAM CONGREVE

ALEXANDRIA AXELROD HUNCHED HER tall body over the bank of computer screens and watched as the file opened up onscreen. Within seconds, she saw what she was looking for.

"Bingo," she said quietly, to no one in particular.

Katie Mahoney wandered over. "Good one?" she asked.

"Listen to this," Alexandria said as she read from the screen. "Dear Sweet Peaches..."

"Sweet Peaches?" Katie laughed.

"That's what it says. Dear Sweet Peaches, I'd love to pick your fruit again soon. Will you be ripe the twentieth at eight p.m.?"

"What's with all the fruit crap?" Katie asked. "Does he tell her he's plucking her cherry each time?"

Katie Mahoney reached into the pocket of her blazer, whipped out her PalmPilot, and brought up her calendar. "Friday the twentieth at eight p.m." she noted as she tapped the screen with the stylus. "Guess I'm not going out on a date that night," she sighed. "And neither are you," she added, knowing full well that it was not likely Alexandria had a date that night, or any other night, for that matter.

Alexandria ignored her as she scanned from screen to screen. Multiple stacks of computers whirred around her, creating a constant low buzz that Alexandria found very comforting. This was their digital operations room, more affectionately called the cybercision center, where the investigators of the Black Widow Agency did the bulk of their computer forensic and analysis work.

Alexandria, known by her teammates as the "Geek Goddess," loved this windowless space. Katie Mahoney hated it. She'd rather work in her own little corner office complete with the wall poster of a shirtless Tom Selleck, and a solid maple desk with a fully loaded forty-millimeter handgun in the top drawer and a fifth of Glenlivet in the bottom drawer.

Just then Margo Norton, their office manager, opened the door. Margo was wearing a flowing, chocolate-colored dress that nearly matched her skin.

"Whatcha y'all up to?" Margo asked as she glanced between the women.

"Planning to tape the next Oscar-award-winning video."

"Well, hold your digital penetrating cameras because y'all have a visitor out here, a Mrs. Gloria Duvay, that's D-U-V-A-Y, who just came in, and she looks pretty damned jammed up, if you ask me."

Alexandria's hands flew across the keyboard as she typed in the name. She tapped another button as the image of a middle-aged woman in a designer suit, sitting in a chair in their conference room, appeared on a screen. The woman glanced nervously around the room. Alexandria zoomed in and quickly grabbed a digital photo of the woman's face for their records.

"Got it," Alexandria called to Katie. "Mrs. Gloria Duvay, DOB 11/14/57 of 14 Abernathy Woods, Langton. Nice neighborhood. Husband is Richard Duvay, president of Du-Tech Architectural Designs. Business has been booming over the last few years. Net earnings up 38 percent over the previous year. Seven-figure bank account on him, no listing on her."

"Sweet Jesus!" Margo exclaimed. "And the only figures I ever see rising are those damned red numbers on that damned scale every morning. Which reminds me, I just made some fresh scones, not that you would care to know," she said flashing her brown eyes at Alexandria and muttering, "damned anorexia poster child," under her breath.

"Thanks, Margo. Settle Mrs. Duvay into the conference room and we'll be right there."

DESPITE THE LARGE, COMFORTABLE chair, Gloria Duvay shifted nervously as the two women walked in. The first woman was tall and model-thin, with short, nearly spiked black hair and dark eyes of almost the same color. Her pale face was expressionless as she strode in and sat down across from Gloria Duvay. When the tall woman crossed her long legs, Gloria couldn't help but notice a small tattoo of a black widow spider on her right inner ankle. The young woman's fingernails were painted dark red, giving her a somewhat gothic appearance.

The other woman was shorter, large-bosomed, and wore a deeply cut blue sweater beneath a linen blazer that was stretched to capacity. She had long, curly blonde hair with reddish highlights, very light blue eyes, and a small nose that reflected her Irish roots. She extended her hand.

"How do you do, Mrs. Duvay," Katie began. "I'm Katie Mahoney, and this is my associate, Alexandria Axelrod."

Alexandria gave a small nod to Gloria Duvay, but didn't smile, didn't offer her hand.

"How can we help you today, Mrs. Duvay?"

Gloria Duvay looked at them both. "My friend Donna Dormond once used your...services...and recommended you."

Katie smiled in recognition. "Of course. And how is Donna?"

"Very well. She just started a new job at a mortgage company, and she's moving to a new home in just a few weeks."

"Excellent," Katie said.

"She wouldn't have been able to afford that—or the Jaguar, or the vacation home—without your help."

"One of the goals of the Black Widow Agency," Katie explained, "is to make sure that the women we serve get what they deserve."

"And that men do, too," Alexandria added quietly.

Katie shot her a look, and Gloria gave a small, nervous laugh.

"So what is it that we can do for you today, Mrs. Duvay?"

"It's my husband, Richard. We've been married for almost twenty-five years. He owns his own business, an architectural firm, which he started from the ground up and has worked hard at for many years. It's one of the leading architectural firms in the area. Perhaps you've heard of it? Du-Tech Architectural Designs?"

Katie nodded to her to go on but didn't give any indication whether she recognized the name or not.

Gloria Duvay continued. "Richard is a wonderful man and a good father to our children, but lately...things just haven't been the same between us, if you know what I mean. He seems rather…distracted."

"I understand," Katie said sympathetically.

"The other night I walked into his den and his computer was turned on. There was an e-mail from a woman named 'BeeBee' that said, 'We're on for the eighteenth at six p.m. Can't wait. Hugs, BeeBee.'"

"Did you notice the return e-mail address?" Alexandria asked.

"No. I heard my husband in the hallway and moved away. I didn't want him to think I was snooping, but I just don't understand what is going on." Gloria Duvay fought back tears.

"This must be such a stressful time for you," Katie said as she leaned forward and lightly touched Gloria Duvay's arm. Without asking, Katie reached over to a side table, picked up the decoupage-covered box of tissues that Margo Norton had made, and offered them to Gloria.

KATIE MAHONEY'S TWELVE YEARS as a cop interviewing people was well spent. She knew every trick of the trade to gain sympathy and trust in people and was capable of looking a pedophile square in the eye and saying, "It must have been so hard for you with all those children around."

"And what would you like us to do for you, Gloria? May I call you Gloria?"

"Yes, of course. I…I guess I'd like you to find out if he's…involved with this woman."

"Very well. We can help you with that," Katie said.

"How will you do it? Find out, I mean."

Katie turned to Alexandria.

"By the time you get home," Alexandria began in a monotone, "you will have received an e-mail from Divinity Chocolates with the subject line of 'free chocolate.' You are to open that e-mail and then delete it."

"That's it?"

"That's it."

Gloria Duvay looked at Alexandria suspiciously. "And what will that do?"

"That will enable what is known as a rootkit invasion on your computer. It will launch a series of other programs, including a keystroke logger. We will then be able to examine the computer, as well as record each and every keystroke made."

"How will I know this…this root thing is there?"

"You won't. The rootkit is designed to operate in stealth mode. It conceals its own presence and instantly disguises itself as other files whenever attempts to detect it are made. It will remain unde-tectable until we remove it."

Gloria Duvay shook her head and said, "But I'm certain he de-leted the e-mail because I looked the next night and it was gone."

"The e-mail is most likely still there," Katie said.

"I don't understand," Gloria Duvay said, confused.

"Let me explain it this way," Katie began. "In school, we had this awful nun, Sister Mary Ignatius."

Gloria Duvay gave a small smile.

"She wouldn't let any of us talk to each other during class or study halls, so we developed a system where we'd write notes to each other in our composition books, but we'd tear off the sheet behind the actual note and pass that along. Of course, if we got

6

caught, it appeared to be a blank page until someone took a pencil to it and rubbed the pencil on its edge to bring up the impression of the original note."

"Yes, I remember doing that," Gloria said.

"Well, that's very much how a computer's hard drive works. Even though the e-mail may have been erased, it isn't really gone. It sits in what's called the slack space of the hard drive for quite some time. Most people think by deleting a file or a message they've gotten rid of it, when in most cases they've just shifted it around. We use state-of-the-art forensic tools to recover those files and messages."

Gloria Duvay shook her head. "I had no idea," she said.

"Most people don't. That's what brought Enron down," Katie said.

"I see. And how will you get these files?"

"We will access it remotely from here."

"You can do that?"

Alexandria smiled for the first time. "In a heartbeat."

"My goodness," Gloria said.

"Pretty amazing, isn't it?" Katie asked. "Incidentally, Alexandria is one of the leading digital security experts in the country. She learned her stuff from the ground up by hacking her way into organizations like the FBI and MicroGage."

Gloria Duvay eyed Alexandria suspiciously.

Alexandria showed no expression when she said, "The FBI was easy. MicroGage took a while."

"And do you still do this?"

"Not since I arrested her," Katie said.

Alexandria watched satisfactorily as the look of shock registered on Gloria Duvay's face.

Gloria Duvay was astounded. "And now you work here, together?"

"Yes. Alexandria discovered that her boyfriend, a fellow hacker, was using his talents to help organized crime syndicates digitally hide and launder billions of dollars, so when she threatened to turn him in, he set her up. He was very clever to leave no evidence to charge him with, but he made sure there was plenty to hang Alex with. The company Alex was caught hacking into was petrified of the public relations debacle it would face if its customer base found out their credit card numbers had been compromised, so they refused to prosecute."

"You were a police officer?" Gloria Duvay asked, giving Katie a quick once-over. Katie laughed.

"Hard to believe, but yes. That's why I was so good at undercover work, because I don't exactly look like a cop. My specialty was undercover narcotics investigations until I realized that the bad guys were using more and more technology to hide evidence, arrange for drop points, solicit children for sex, launder money, etc. I started one of the first computer crime and computer forensics units in the state. The state police now have their own division, but the backlog of computers that need to be examined is three years long because they're so poorly funded. Unfortunately, cases are being dropped because they can't process the evidence quickly enough.

"I was working undercover, trying to penetrate an illegal drug ring, when I found out that my husband, who was a fellow police officer, was having an affair. When I filed for divorce, my real identity was somehow leaked," Katie paused, "which almost cost me my life. As if getting shot wasn't bad enough, I was accused of tampering with evidence in a case and got kicked off the force. I lost my pension and my benefits."

"And your ex-husband?"

"He was promoted to captain a few months ago."

"He didn't get punished for it?"

"The police department did its own internal investigation and every officer that possibly could have been interviewed was. Needless to say, the internal investigation was closed out as 'unfounded.' No one produced any information. That's okay," Katie said as she glanced at Alexandria, "sometimes justice takes a little longer."

Gloria Duvay shook her head.

"Then there's our office manager, Margo Norton," Katie went on. "Her husband once asked her to deliver a backpack to someone but neglected to tell her it contained cocaine."

"Dear heavens," Gloria said.

"I arrested her as soon as she handed the package over to me. She's now raising their young son alone. Our finance director, Jane Landers, has an ex-husband who insisted throughout their forty-one years of marriage that she wasn't even capable of paying their bills. She earned her CPA degree after he took all their money and his girlfriend to Bermuda. Bermuda refuses to extradite." Katie paused. "So you see, Gloria, we have all been wronged by our men in one way or another. That's why we fight so hard to make it right for women."

"My goodness," Gloria Duvay said, "you must all hate men."

Katie glanced at Alexandria for just a second before answering, "Not at all. We just despise the type of man who thinks he can dump on women and get away with it. We fight back by gathering evidence, utilizing the latest technologies in computer forensics and high-tech surveillance equipment. That equipment accounts for 50 percent of our resources."

"What's the other 50 percent?" Gloria Duvay asked.

"Women's intuition," Katie answered.

A FEW WEEKS LATER, the three women sat in the conference room and watched as the video played on the big screen. As they watched, Margo passed the plate of chocolate, their favorite movie snack. "Oh yeah, he's popping her cherry all right," Margo said.

"Gives new meaning to the words 'Cling Peaches'," replied Katie.

"You white girls sure can bend a lot," Margo said and they both laughed.

Alexandria watched the screen with intense silence as she lightly stroked the back of her pet tarantula, Divinity. Meanwhile, Jane covered the front desk as, out of modesty, she preferred not to participate in the video screenings.

"Look! I think he's trying to make a peach cobbler or something," Katie said and Margo burst out laughing. Katie popped a chocolate truffle into her mouth.

"You think those big mangos are real?" Margo asked as Katie passed the platter back. Margo offered it to Alexandria but she declined as usual.

"I don't know about those mangos, but I think his banana's about to be peeled and he's taking two full cups of Peptobimbo to boot." Katie stood up and mimicked the action on screen. "Pluck me, you cherry picker, pluck me, pluck me. Yesssss, yesssss, yesssss!"

Margo doubled up in laughter. "That's one flexible Ho TOW all right," she said.

They used the acronym TOW for "The Other Woman." A "High TOW" was a woman well-kept by a lover replete with housing and expense money. A "Working TOW" was a working woman only in it for sex. A "Ho TOW" was a woman who, in their collective opinions, was comparable to a streetwalker.

"That girl's a regular 7-Eleven," Margo said.

"Huh?"

"Open all night, good to go, and for ninety-nine cents you can get a Slurpee."

Just then, Jane knocked on the door. Alexandria quickly hit the button on the remote to stop the video.

Jane glanced nervously toward the screen. "Excuse me, Katie, but Mrs. Duvay is back to see you," she said. They all stood up and Alexandria hit another button to retract the screen. Mahogany panels automatically slid into place to cover it.

Margo slipped into the kitchen to make a fresh pot of coffee.

"Have you decided what you're going to tell her?" Alexandria asked.

Katie checked herself in the small mirror of the compact she carried that doubled as a wireless video camera. "I'll know when I see her," she answered.

THE CONFERENCE ROOM OF the Black Widow Agency was specifically designed by Margo Norton to be as welcoming as possible to the many women who would become their clients. Margo's decorating talents were a family affair. Her twin brother, Marcus, and his partner, Antoine, were co-owners of one of the hottest interior decorating firms in the Northeast, "Sachet and Sashay." Their offices were located in the other half of the renovated building that had once served as a law office. Marcus and Antoine, in collaboration with Margo, provided much of the interior design ideas and in return, Katie and Alexandria provided them with computer and technical support whenever needed.

Twins Margo and Marcus had had several "family discussions," as Katie called them, "bitch slapping" Margo termed it, over choosing just the right wallpaper for the conference room. They finally agreed on a heavily textured, sage-green paper with raised leaves throughout. The woodwork was all mahogany. The lighting was soft, the chairs comfortable. Fresh coffee steamed in a pot along with warm muffins or scones that Margo made every morning just after putting her son, Trevor, on the school bus. Every day Margo produced a fresh flower arrangement so the room always smelled floral and feminine.

The bar in the back of the conference room was kept well stocked for the times when the news they had to deliver warranted something stronger than coffee. Lately, their clients had been hitting the liquor cabinet quite often.

GLORIA DUVAY WATCHED AS the two women came into the room. The tall, dark, expressionless one sat down directly across from her and folded her pencil-thin legs. The well-endowed blonde sat in a chair at an angle.

"How are you today, Gloria?" Katie asked, reaching out to shake her hand.

"A little nervous."

"Don't be. Would you like a drink?" Katie asked as she undid the thick file in her lap.

Gloria eyed the file nervously, aware that it held secrets that would ultimately determine her future. "No, thank you," she said.

Katie took out several papers and cleared her throat. "At your request we engaged in a digital penetration of your home computer to determine your husband's activities relative to a female subject by the name of 'Bee-Bee.'"

Alexandria watched Gloria Duvay intently, her hands quietly clasped in her lap.

Katie flipped back her long, reddish-blonde hair and tapped the file.

"This is a most unusual case, Gloria, and I'm somewhat at a loss to know how much to say," she said.

"What do you mean?" Gloria asked.

Katie leaned forward in her chair. "Gloria, Bee-Bee is actually Beatrice Waterson, the owner of 'Busy as a Bee Party Planners.'"

Gloria Duvay blinked. "He's having an affair with a party planner?" she asked.

"No, Gloria. He's not having an affair, he's planning an affair."

"I don't understand."

"Didn't you say you and Richard have been married for almost twenty-five years?"

Katie watched as her words sunk in. Gloria's mouth dropped open, her face relaxed, and her eyes started to well up. She immediately covered her mouth with her hand.

"Oh my word, you mean he's planning a surprise anniversary party?"

"Yes, but you see, now we've ruined the surprise…"

Gloria Duvay cried. Katie whipped out the tissue box. Gloria grabbed several tissues and dabbed at her eyes.

"All this time, I thought he was, you know…Things between us just haven't been the same lately so I thought…I feel so foolish now."

"You shouldn't," Katie said. "Unfortunately, most times a woman's worst suspicions are correct."

"When I saw the e-mail about the eighteenth and meeting her, I just assumed…"

Katie reached into the file.

"Gloria, I want you to hear more of that e-mail." She cleared her throat while she read from the printout. "While I do not have an unlimited budget, Bee-Bee, I want this to be a very special evening for a very special lady. For twenty-five years she's put up with me and that, in itself, deserves a great deal of recognition." Katie slipped the paper back in the file. "There's more, but I think we've ruined enough of the surprise already."

Gloria dabbed away at her cheeks. "Oh, thank you. Thank you both so much," she said as she stood up and hugged Katie. She turned toward Alexandria, but Alex merely waved at her and said, "Good luck to you." Gloria Duvay awkwardly waved back.

"On your way out, we'll have you settle your account with Jane," Katie said gently.

"Oh, yes of course. And thank you again, so much. I can't begin to tell you what a relief this is."

Before she left, Alexandria reached over to the small table and picked up a covered silver dish. "Would you like to celebrate with a chocolate?" she asked quietly, her black eyes flashing.

"Why, yes, thank you."

Alexandria, who always derived a great deal of pleasure from this moment, whisked the cover off and watched as Gloria gasped and withdrew her hand.

"Goodness," she said, "I thought they were real."

"I know," Alexandria said as she looked down admiringly at the pile of chocolates cleverly shaped like black widow spiders, complete with small red roses on their backs.

"On second thought, I think I'll pass."

Disappointed, Alexandria took one and popped it whole into her mouth.

Katie escorted Gloria Duvay to Jane Landers' office.

At sixty-one years old, Jane Landers was the oldest of the four women who made up the Black Widow Agency. Her dull gray hair was cut short and though no one had the heart to say so, they suspected she cut it herself, the back often looking ragged. She rarely wore makeup and dressed in the comfort of elastic-waist polyester slacks with coordinating tops—largely acquired, they could tell from the tags, at the nearest giant retailer. It was not that Jane was unattractive. Her eyes were an unusual shade of green that Katie suspected were quite fetching at one time. She was simply the kind of woman you'd least remember. Despite her unadorned appearance, Jane was a financial whiz who not only kept the books of the Black Widow Agency, but also assisted on any investigations involving corporate fraud, embezzlement, money laundering, or any other financial schemes they happened to come upon.

Jane's office space was a memorial to her one-year-old grand-daughter, MaryJane. Pictures of MaryJane at birth, and every month afterward, adorned the walls of her office. MaryJane lived with Jane's daughter, Alice and her husband, about an hour away in Boston. Though Jane offered to go down and help Alice every weekend, they rarely took her up on the offers, although no one at the agency had the heart to point this out to Jane. So it was that despite her grandchild being an hour away, Jane saw her only oc-casionally—living vicariously through the numerous digital pho-tos and e-mails detailing MaryJane's progress, which Alice sent her way.

Katie led Gloria Duvay in and tapped on Jane's door. She could see that Jane was in the midst of one of her hot flashes, which seemed like a part-time job lately. Jane kept a small fan pointed toward her as she dabbed a cool cloth on her glistening forehead.

Jane quickly set the damp cloth aside on a nearby plate.

"Mrs. Duvay would like to settle her account."

"Yes, of course," she said, rising. Jane extended her hand as she welcomed Gloria Duvay.

"They're miserable, those hot flashes, aren't they?" Gloria Du-vay offered as she shook Jane's hand.

Jane nodded. "I suppose I should think of them as power surges, but lately I feel like I'm going to self-combust."

Gloria Duvay, who was feeling quite happy at that moment, said, "My friend told me a joke the other day: with the onset of hot flashes, our memory starts to go and the only thing we're able to retain is water." Glancing around Jane's office, Gloria noted the abundant museum of photos. "Is that your granddaughter?" she asked.

Jane beamed and picked up the first of what Katie knew would be a succession of framed photos and passed it over.

"That's my little MaryJane. She's almost a year old now."

KATIE ROLLED HER EYES. She left the two women alone, but paused long enough to watch through the glass side panels as Gloria took out a thick envelope and began counting out a large stack of one-hundred-dollar bills. Satisfied, Katie walked back to the conference room. As she passed Margo's desk, Margo looked up from her decorating magazine and asked, "Did she bite?"

"Alex whipped off the lid at ninety miles an hour again and she freaked."

"I'll kill the damn bitch," Margo said, because it was she who labored for hours over double-boilers to produce their trademark chocolates.

KATIE WALKED BACK INTO the conference room to find Alexandria still sitting in the chair, waiting for her.

"You want a drink?" Katie asked as she approached the bar.

"It's not even eleven AM," Alexandria observed.

"Somewhere in the world it's eleven PM," Katie said as she poured scotch in a glass and knocked it back in one gulp. She could feel Alexandria's dark eyes on her the whole time.

"Okay, what is it?" Katie asked as she plopped down in the chair that Gloria Duvay had just occupied. She reached down and scratched at her ankle near her own black widow spider tattoo. They all had them except Jane who, in deference to her age, preferred not to "mutilate her body."

"Why didn't you tell her?" Alexandria asked.

"Why should I?"

"Because it's the truth."

"She hired us to find out if her husband was having an affair with that woman. He isn't. So what if he gets off looking at pictures of nude guys in collars? We satisfied our contractual obligations."

"You don't think he has some guy stashed somewhere?"

"I don't know, but the point is that they still care about each other. I'd like to think some man cared about me after twenty-five years of being together," she said.

"Wouldn't we all."

Katie stood up. "And by the way, Margo's pissed that you whipped the cover off the chocolates again."

"I did no such thing," Alexandria said.

"Bullshit," Katie stated.

Katie reached over and grabbed the lid of the silver tray. "You whipped it off like this," she said as she quickly pulled the cover off. "Jesus, Mary, and Joseph!" she yelled, with a slight trace of a brogue. One of the spiders was moving. "For Christ's sakes, Alex, do you have to put that thing in there?"

Alexandria laughed as she reached over and scooped up the small fuzzy tarantula in her hands. "Come here, Divinity," she said affectionately. "Auntie Katie doesn't love you anymore." She brought

19

the small spider to her lips and kissed it. Katie watched in disgust as the tarantula reached its legs out toward Alexandria's mouth.

"The deal was you were supposed to keep that thing in its cage," Katie said, brushing her hair back.

"No creature wants to be caged all the time," Alexandria said as she let her pet crawl across her very flat chest.

SHORTLY AFTER KATIE MADE the rank of detective, she was put in charge of the Laketon Police Department's first computer forensic division. Her job was to deal with the increasing amount of electronic crime. The supervisors deemed Katie a computer whiz based solely on the fact that she seemed to be the only one who could clear the frequently jammed copier machine; but, in fact, she did have a talent for computers. Shortly after acquiring one of the earliest computer forensic workstations for the department, she received an e-mail from an anonymous source about a hacker known in the underworld community of hackers as the "Geek Goddess." This "Geek Goddess" was alleged to be using keystroke loggers, covert programs that recorded keystrokes, to gain entry into a leading corporation that held databases of security numbers, credit card numbers, and bank account numbers on millions of customers. The tipster gave such detailed information about this Geek Goddess, including her real name, Alexandria Axelrod, that Katie was quite certain the relationship must be a personal one, if in fact the information was legitimate. The incriminating documents the tipster attached to the anonymous e-mail consisted of page after page of bank account transactions. Each transaction was for under two hundred dollars, which Katie knew would easily go unnoticed considering all of the accounts that had been pilfered had six-figure balances at a minimum. What baffled her completely was that the transactions all went to a number of charitable organizations, including the American Cancer Society, the Children's Leukemia Fund, and a number of other children's organizations. Katie called it her "Cyber Robin Hood" case and began an investigation. All attempts to run background traces on the suspect, Alexandria Axelrod, produced nothing. There was no credit history, no educational history, not even a parking ticket. The only documentation Katie came up with was a valid driver's license. The original e-mail itself had been sent through "anonymizers" on the Internet that made its source untraceable.

With no other way to reach out to her, Katie began surveillance on the suspect. For a week she watched an apartment in a moderately priced, contemporary complex and saw little activity other than an occasional light being turned on. She knew the suspect or someone was in the apartment but rarely emerged.

On the day she set out to execute the search warrant, Katie made sure she had additional backup units with her because she was concerned they might be walking into a trap. The plan was for a three AM takedown because it was safest to execute the warrant while the suspect was sound asleep. Little did they expect upon entering the premises to find the suspect not only wide awake, but fully dressed.

She was sitting in front of a blank computer screen sipping a diet soda as if she had been expecting them all along. Katie looked curiously at the young, dark-haired, thin-as-a-rail woman. She showed almost no reaction as the six officers, with guns drawn, searched from room to room of her apartment. She simply nodded when

Katie asked her if she was Alexandria Axelrod. That's when Katie realized the computer screen was blank because the hard drive had been securely wiped clean. "Damn," Katie said to herself. Another monitor suddenly beeped and came to life. Katie saw the image of one of her fellow officers pop-up on the screen as he moved around outside the premises and realized there had been absolutely nothing covert about their operation. Alexandria Axelrod had been watching their every move by a system of closed circuit cameras mounted at the front door and every window.

They seized all of her equipment, but the computer's hard drive was obliterated. Katie brought the woman into an interview room. The interrogation was pointless. The suspect said very little other than a request for a diet soda.

"Alexandria, you're not making this any easier on yourself," Katie pointed out as she sat facing the twenty-two-year-old across the old wooden desk. "These are serious charges and you could be facing federal time. It would be in your best interest to cooperate. Trust me on this," Katie said. "You must be feeling very frightened right now. Let me help you." She waited but got no response. She'd never met a more frustrating suspect to interview. The only change in expression came when Katie asked, "Do you have any idea where we got all this information?"

Alexandria Axelrod winced for all of a second and Katie caught it. "It was someone close, wasn't it, Alexandria?" she asked. The suspect turned her head ever so slightly.

"It would be so much easier if you could explain that," Katie asked, more out of curiosity than concern. Again, she got no response. She tried another tactic and brought out the copies of the transactions. She placed them in front of the suspect.

"Why all the charities?" She watched as the woman stared intently at the papers.

"Is there any family you want to call?"

"No."

"No one? A boyfriend, perhaps?" She caught the wince again and Katie knew for certain that it was a boyfriend who set this young woman up. She almost felt bad for her, but she had her job to do.

THREE HOURS LATER WHEN the sun rose and the city came to life, Katie marched into the corporate headquarters of the company whose information Alexandria Axelrod had pillaged. Katie knew that the evidence and chance of prosecution was sketchy at best without their full cooperation and testimony. The company president, a man who spoke more like a politician than a businessman, announced abruptly that under no circumstances were they going to cooperate or press charges against this young woman. Katie couldn't believe her ears. The director of information technologies, who was responsible for their network security, sat next to the company president and gulped repeatedly, knowing his days with the company were likely numbered by the breach. The president explained to Katie that they could not afford the negative publicity should their clientele realize their information had been compromised. Katie pleaded with him to reconsider and pointed out that a criminal offense had been committed, but the effort was futile. She drove back to the station in a daze. When she got back, she tried in vain to explain the case to her captain, who was clueless about computers, to see if there were any other options for prosecution. There were none.

Without tipping her hand, she walked down to the holding cells and released Alexandria. As Alexandria walked away from the police station, Katie ran out after her.

"Alexandria, wait!"

Alexandria turned and looked at her curiously.

"Look, how about we go get a cup of coffee and then I'll drive you home?" Katie offered.

"Why?" Alexandria asked.

"Because I…" Katie hesitated. There was no point in lying, the case was closed with "insufficient evidence to pursue" stamped across it. "Because I'd like to know how you did it," Katie said as honestly as she could. The woman nodded and Katie drove them to a nearby coffeehouse.

Before exiting the car, Katie slipped her badge off of her belt and made sure Alexandria saw her stash it in the glove compartment. "We're off the record now, understood?" The young woman nodded.

"You knew we were coming," Katie said peering at her as she sipped her black coffee.

"Yes."

"And you had everything triggered to wipe clean."

"Yes."

"You understand you're a free woman and you're welcome to walk out that door right now?" Katie said pointing.

"Yes."

Katie took a sip of the steaming coffee. "Alexandria, who did this to you?"

Alexandria Axelrod showed little emotion as she spoke. "He must have known that I was about to turn him in," she said.

"Who?"

"A guy. Just some guy I was…involved with."

"What were you going to turn him in for?"

"Money laundering."

"On the 'net?"

"Yes."

"Who's he working for?"

The woman hesitated. "The mob."

Katie came to attention. "Is there any evidence?"

Alexandria gave a small laugh. "No, and there never will be. I can guarantee you that. I was the only one who would ever have been able to get any evidence on him."

"And now it's gone?"

Alexandria nodded. "He got to me before I could get to him," she said with a trace of disappointment.

"Would you be willing to testify to any of this?"

"No."

"Why not?"

"What difference would it make? It would be my word against his, and now I have a record with the police. That was his point."

Katie watched her carefully. "Did you care about him?" she asked.

Again, she saw the briefest glint of pain. Alexandria paused for some time before responding. "I thought I did and I thought he cared for me, but obviously I was wrong." Alexandria rose. "I'd like to go home now," she said.

"Wait," Katie said, reaching out for her arm. Alexandria immediately recoiled away from her. Katie withdrew her hand and kept her distance. Alexandria reluctantly sat back down. "You know what I think?" Katie said. "I think this guy really meant something to you and maybe for the first time in your life, you let your guard down."

Alexandria stared with no emotion.

"I think you cared very much for him and maybe you're not only hurting but a little pissed off that someone one-upped you."

Alexandria stood up again. "I'd like to go home now," she said again.

Katie had found that single point of vulnerability and pounced as she was so capable of doing. "All of these accounts you've dipped into and donated to charities—it's because deep-down you care about people. I've heard about people like you; you use your talents to play Cyber Robin Hood, all the while justifying in your mind that it was for a good cause—but it's still against the law. It must have been incredibly painful for you to realize that you had to end that relationship…" She paused but got absolutely no reaction. "You told him you were ending it and he got pissed off and maybe even nasty with you, so you did what you had to do. You started gathering evidence. You figured you'd outsmart him at his own game, but he got the goods on you first and took you down instead. You must be incredibly angry. I know I would be."

"I'm going home now," Alexandria said, walking away.

THEY SAID NO MORE until they got back to Alexandria's apartment. As Alexandria reached for the door handle, Katie once again instinctively reached for her arm, but checked herself. "Alexandria, I'm still new at all this computer stuff and there's a lot I need to learn. Do you suppose I could reach out to you if I ever get stuck on a case?"

Alexandria gave her a small nod and closed the door.

SO IT BEGAN THAT when Katie needed greater technical expertise on a case, she would quietly consult Alexandria, who not only could answer every question, but sometimes would even deliver the evidence without Katie knowing how she obtained it. Since no one else in the department knew the first thing about computer forensics, few questions were asked and even fewer answers were given. In time, Katie and Alexandria developed a relationship based on mutual respect.

With Alexandria's knowledge and covert assistance, Katie went deeper and deeper into the world of keystroke loggers, backdoor entries, trojan viruses, phishing, and the underworld of cyber hacking. She soon came to realize that the bad guys were far ahead of the good guys in using technology. She uncovered money laundering schemes, drug trafficking schemes, and identity theft.

Using what Alexandria taught her, Katie assumed an untraceable covert identity and used the Internet to arrange for illegal drug buys. The buys were small and, although witnessed by other undercover detectives, they often chose not to take the dealer down, opting instead to bargain with them to go up the food chain to an even bigger dealer. Katie arranged on-line to meet the dealers, then drove out to abandoned warehouses, fishing piers, and back alleys to make the deals. Her captain realized how much further she had been able to penetrate the ring of drug dealers than any of his more seasoned narcotics detectives and gave her full rein. The more successful she became in making the undercover buys, the more she craved the whole experience. The adrenaline rush was addictive. She came home, when she came home, so hyped up that the only way to take the edge off the constant rush was by knocking back a few glasses of scotch. Joe Kennedy, Katie's husband and a fellow police officer, had been assigned to midnights so they rarely saw each other. When they did, she was usually near-drunk.

The day before Katie was on the verge of making the biggest undercover cocaine buy in the department's history, she and Joe had a terrible fight. She had heard the rumors around the department about Joe having an affair, but was so focused on her own work that she wrote them off as petty jealousy. Still, the rumors were out there. In the course of a raging fight, she drunkenly asked Joe if it was true. He admitted everything, denied nothing. He pleaded with her to forgive him, explained how lonely he was, confessed that he still loved her, but she had somehow changed. In her enraged drunken state, Katie kicked Joe out and told him she was filing for divorce. She drank more that night than ever before.

The next night, when the drug deal was to go down, she was miserably hung over and about as sharp as a cotton ball. She drank cup after cup of black coffee and knew going into the deal that she was in no shape for it, but counted on the adrenaline to kick in and sharpen her senses. As was always the case, she went to the location carrying no weapons, no badge. This was for her own safety in case she got frisked, which she often did. The deal went down in a dead-end alley that gave her little cover protection for her backup units. Katie, who had some of the best instincts in the business, threw up before arriving for the tactical pre-op meeting. The captain noted the green tinge to her skin and yanked her aside to quietly ask her if she was okay. Everything in her gut told her not to go, but she still went.

PAUL WYKOFF WAS ONLY twenty-five years old, yet one of the most successful drug dealers in the state. He worked only under cover of darkness and never directly sold to the public, only to other dealers, threatening their lives and their families' lives should they ever turn on him. He was street smart and fearless.

The deal with Wykoff went down smoothly, much to Katie's relief. The exchange was made in a poorly lit alley with no traffic. As soon as Katie turned around to walk back to her car with three kilos of cocaine stuffed in a backpack, she heard a sound she recognized that made her freeze in her tracks. It was the racking of a slide on a handgun as a bullet slid into the chamber. She turned and a nine-millimeter was shoved in her stomach. An arm was thrown tightly around her neck and the gun placed to the side of her ribs.

"She gets it if anyone comes near us," Wykoff called out loudly. Katie saw movement on a nearby rooftop. It was one of her backups, but Wykoff was so close to her she could smell his breath and she knew they'd never get a clear shot.

"What the fuck?" she asked trying to feign innocence.

"You'd better tell your cop friends to back off!" he said. "Tell them!"

Her breathing got hard and fast and for the first time that night, her senses kicked into full force. She caught the tiniest of movement from behind a garbage can to her right and realized one of her backups was right behind it, no more than twelve feet away.

"Tell them!" Wykoff screamed at her again. With as much weight as Katie could muster, she shoved him aside and instinctively screamed "Gun!" at the top of her lungs. Her screams were heightened by the sensation of intense heat ripping through her abdomen. She clutched at her side and fell to the pavement just as she saw one of her fellow detectives discharge his weapon at Wykoff. The vision of Wykoff's head slamming full force back onto the pavement was the last image etched in her mind until she woke up in a hospital fourteen hours later. Wykoff also survived.

KATIE WALKED INTO THE offices of the Black Widow Agency to hear raised voices emanating from their conference room. She slowly opened the door.

"It's mauve!" Marcus said, placing his hands firmly on his hips.

"I still say it's taupe," Antoine answered back quietly.

Marcus dramatically put both his hands to his cheeks. Each finger sported a large, glittery ring. "I don't believe this," he said. "I'm engaged to a man who doesn't even know the difference between mauve and taupe." He shook his head in disgust.

Katie slipped in and went over to Margo. "What's going on?" she whispered.

"Lover's quarrel."

"It has the undertones of lavender, therefore it's mauve," Marcus said.

"Hey, you guys," Katie said, trying to divert their attention.

"Katarina, darling," Marcus said as he strode over to kiss her on both cheeks. He stopped short and stepped back to assess her outfit. He looked aghast. "My God, darling, where ever did you get that atrocity, L.L. Boring?"

Katie smiled. Marcus was in his trademark lavender silk slacks and wore a yellow mesh sweater over that. Antoine, as always, wore a long black shirt over black silk pants and sandals. Marcus made a "tsk, tsk" sound between his teeth as he poked at Katie's breasts. "With these lovelies, you should be dressing faboo, not hagoo, darling."

"So what's going on?" Katie asked.

"This one!" Marcus said, pointing to Antoine. "He's color blind. Imagine an interior designer who is color blind!"

Defeated, Antoine sat in the chair next to Alexandria, who was also dressed head to toe in black. He looked over admiringly at Divinity, who was resting on Alexandria's knee.

"May I touch her?" he asked softly. With the tiniest of nods, Alexandria gave him permission. He very gently touched one of Divinity's legs. "She's pretty," he said.

"Oh Lord, have mercy," Marcus said in complete exasperation. "You're not bringing one of those home, Antoine, so don't even think about it." He turned to Katie. "It simply does not go with the motif," he said. Shaking his head with exasperation, he said quietly, "He drives me wild. He must be cycling again." Lifting his martini glass, he said, "Katarina, darling, join me, will you?"

Katie sniffed at his drink. "What've you got there, Marcus?" she asked.

"This little gem," he began as he sipped, "is made of sweet vermouth, dry sherry, and orange bitters." He peered over the glass as he said, "It's called an Adonis cocktail. I'm not sure which I like better, the drink or the name." He flashed his brown eyes at her.

Katie smiled, poured herself some scotch and sat down in one of the large, upholstered chairs. She savored the golden malty liquid on her tongue for a few seconds before letting it slide slowly down the back of her throat. The combination of peaty and smoky flavors warmed her instantly.

KATIE WAS PROUD OF how well the office space had turned out, even if it cost a fortune. Neither Jane nor Margo knew that most of the funding for the building came from Alexandria. She seemed to have bottomless resources, but money was one topic she and Katie rarely discussed—the agreement being that Katie would not ask any questions, nor would she stop Alexandria from acquiring the endless barrage of gadgets and equipment that was constantly delivered to them.

But nothing compared to their restroom, dubbed the "Bain de Femme" by Marcus. When Marcus and Antoine designed it, Marcus insisted they put a full shower in, which, to everyone's surprise, was used far more than anyone had anticipated. The shower was made of Moroccan tile. Two full-length mirrors set into a corner gave a three-dimensional view, something Katie wasn't always sure she liked, especially since at the age of thirty-eight, her once flat stomach had softened. The sinks of copper were recessed in rust-colored marble counters that made them appear to float in air. The vanity had wraparound mirrors with simulated natural lighting and soft chairs to sit at and apply makeup. The best part, they all agreed, was the small device that automatically put the lid down on the toilet each time it was used. Margo called it "the best damned little craphouse in town."

The Black Widow Agency offices were located in southern New Hampshire, just north of Boston, where many of their clients hailed from. There were two separate entrances in the front of the building, one for the Black Widow Agency and one for Marcus and Antoine's business, Sachet and Sashay. The only common area between the two was the kitchen, which both Margo and her brother Marcus insisted they needed. Although Katie initially balked at the idea of spending money on a kitchen at a business, she soon realized the advantages when, upon returning from a late-night surveillance, they'd find some of Margo's delicious gourmet treats in the refrigerator waiting for them. The kitchen was also their "Case Closed" celebration room, where at the end of each case, Margo would whip up something to signify their success—the only mutually agreed-upon requirement that chocolate be a key ingredient.

KATIE WAS JUST ABOUT to pour herself another scotch when Jane opened the door.

"Excuse me, Katie," Jane said, "there's a young lady out here who would like to speak to someone."

Marcus stood up and reached a hand out to Antoine. "Come, Adonis," he said. "These spider women must get to work." Giving Antoine a good once-over, he added, "I think you and I have our own undercover work to do."

Marcus leaned over to Margo and kissed her on both cheeks, saying, "Ta ta, sweet sister."

Margo rolled her eyes. "Ta ta, my ass," Margo hissed back.

Jane waited for Marcus and Antoine to slip out through the kitchen before saying, "Her name is Amber Gordon and she looks pretty upset."

"Stall her for just a minute, Janie, will you?" Katie said.

"Poor girl," Margo said as soon as Jane walked out. "Let's hope she doesn't scare her away with two thousand photos of Princess MaryJane."

Alexandria slipped into the cybercision center and quickly typed the name into a customized search engine while manipulating the zoom lens of a camera in the main lobby to capture the woman's face. "Amber Gordon, age thirty-one, MIT grad, fifth in her class, graduated with a B.S. in Automotive Engineering," she called out as Katie sprayed her mouth with mint freshener. "She got a nice write-up in an article about young female engineers in nontraditional fields." Katie glanced briefly at the article.

AMBER GORDON NERVOUSLY CLUTCHED the teacup Margo had brought her. Her blonde hair was pulled back flat to her head in a very contemporary style, something Katie's thick curly hair would never allow her to do. Amber Gordon had deep circles under her blue eyes.

"My friend, Barbara Biloxi, recommended I come see you," she explained. "We used to live in the same neighborhood in Hyde Park."

"And how is Barbara doing?" Katie asked.

"Very well. She's going on vacation to the timeshare in Aruba... again. She said she wouldn't have that if it hadn't been for your agency's help."

"And the ex?"

"He was with that…that woman…up until a month ago, but she dumped him after he lost all his money. From what Barbara said, someone stole his identity, wiped out his bank account, and trashed all of his credit."

Without a glance at Alexandria, Katie said, "Really? How unfortunate."

Amber tried to sip the tea but her hands shook so badly, she set the cup back down.

"I can see you're very nervous, Amber. Please don't be," Katie said gently. "We're here to help you."

"That's the problem. I don't know if you can help me. No one else has been able to."

"What is it that you need help with, Amber?"

"I want you to get my daughter back."

"I WAS OFFERED A full scholarship to MIT and graduated fifth in my class, the only female automotive engineering major. I was raised with a strong work ethic from working-class parents who encouraged me to do my best. While I was at MIT, I met and fell in love with a fellow automotive engineering student. Upon graduation, Anthony and I went to work at Sumner Design, an automotive parts designer and manufacturer. I was offered a position as a junior engineer. I started working there the day after I graduated. As I'm sure you can gather, it's a predominantly male field.

"I worked fourteen-hour days, six days a week, and did what I had to do to get the job done. There were a few women who worked at Sumner Design in the human resources and accounting departments, but I was the only female engineer. I was raised with three brothers and know what guys are like, so I put up with all the jokes and come-ons and didn't say anything because I wanted to get ahead and prove that I could be 'one of the boys.'"

Katie nodded with complete understanding.

"In the beginning, it was harmless stuff, but gross. They'd have…" she paused and looked at them apologetically, "belching competitions every Friday after lunch. It was mostly that kind of juvenile stuff, but then it started to get worse. They would place pushpins on their office cubicles to signify sexual conquests. Of course, some of them put them there when we all knew they weren't really getting any, but they'd still slap each other on the back and give each other high-fives. Then they made up a system where the colors meant things. A red pushpin meant the girl was 'hot.' A white one meant she was a virgin.

"I'd be working in my cubicle and could hear their laughter all around. Then they started downloading porn videos from the Internet and they'd all stand around and watch them and cheer the whole thing on. Some days I'd turn my own computer on and my screensaver would have been changed to one with nude women in leather with whips."

Katie shook her head. "Did you ever complain about it?" she asked.

"I mentioned it to Anthony and he said something to the president of the company. The next thing you know, everyone was dragged into diversity training, where I was the only woman present with all of the guys who were doing these things. The facilitator was a guy. It was very uncomfortable, and afterward everyone made fun of the training like it was a big joke. Some of the guys

I worked with would come up to me after that and before they'd speak, they'd drop their heads and say very fast, 'I apologize in advance if I offend you in any way,' and then they would say something absolutely offensive anyway."

"What was Anthony's attitude toward all this?" Katie asked.

Amber shook her head. "When it was just Anthony and I alone, he wasn't like them, at least not in the beginning. As time went on, he started acting more like them when he was with the guys. He planned on moving up the corporate ladder, so for his own selfish reasons, he didn't want me to say anything."

Katie shook her head. "What about the other women?" Katie asked.

"Every Christmas, Donald Sumner, the president of the company, would dress up as Santa Claus, bring all the women into his office, sit them on his lap and ask them if they'd been 'good girls' that year. Then he'd hand over a very large bonus check. One year, a young woman complained about getting groped by an engineer and her bonus was half of what the other women got, so the message was very clear not to say anything. It was a big bonus and a lot of these women were single moms who counted on that check to make it through the year.

"I tried not to let it bother me and stay focused on my work. I simply wanted to get some attention for all the hard work I was putting in; however, after the diversity training incident, I realized that the other engineers were getting the 'hot' jobs, while I was still getting junk work."

"What do you mean by that?" Katie said interrupting.

"The big ticket in automotive design is anything to do with the body of the car. That's what gets noticed the most. From an engineering standpoint, body design is the sexy part that builds an engineer's reputation. I tried several times to submit body style designs but they would just smile at me and say, 'That's very nice, Amber, now why don't you go back to your little cubby and see if you can redesign this door handle.' It was so frustrating because I knew my designs were good, but I couldn't get anyone to even look at them.

"Needless to say, this put a huge strain on our marriage. I began to complain more and more to Anthony, which didn't help. I thought Anthony loved me. I know his family didn't, which made it even worse. The first time I met his mother, she made it clear that I wasn't 'one of them' because I came from working class. After we got married, she pretty much told me it was my job to stay at home and take care of Anthony. I didn't need that on top of what was happening at work."

"Of course not," Katie said sympathetically.

"We had a lot of fights, but then we'd make up and I thought everything was okay. When I got pregnant we were both thrilled, absolutely thrilled. His mother even let up on me for a while. That was probably the best time in our marriage. We bought the land in Hyde Park and I set out to design our house. I poured my heart and soul into the design of that house. I'm not a licensed architect, so we still had to hire one to sign off on the plans, but I designed the entire house myself. I used all of my engineering skills to make it special, make it unique, make it our home. I loved it so much that I actually considered going back to school for an architectural degree. Designing houses isn't all that different from designing cars. The mechanics and size may be different, but they still need to be efficient and beautiful, a marriage of form and function. I was responsible for every detail of the design from the type of heating system to the color of the stain on the molding. Anthony never said much about it.

"When the baby was born, life was good for a while. I had a beautiful, healthy daughter and a gorgeous house that others were always admiring. Everything was fine until I told Anthony I was ready to go back to work because I missed designing. He said he thought I would stay home and take care of the baby. We had never really discussed it much, but I loved designing. I mean I love my daughter, but I love what I do, too, so I arranged for the best child-care available and returned to work.

"His mother was absolutely appalled. She accused me of 'abandoning my baby' and told me I should be ashamed of myself. No matter what I did from then on, she found fault with me. It put a huge strain on our relationship."

"I'm sure it did," Katie said as Margo came in to refill Amber's teacup.

Amber paused for a moment to look around the room. "This is a really great space," she observed. "Very staid, classy, but functional. I love the colors—muted, soft, yet powerful in a way."

Margo beamed.

"And this is the lady we all owe it to," Katie said. "This is Margo. She's the one with all the decorating talent."

"Well done," Amber said.

"It's a damned curse, but someone's got to keep up appearances," Margo replied.

Amber smiled.

"When I returned to work, things got worse. I was assigned to the lowest-level projects and given unreasonable deadlines. I took as much work as I could home with me, but with the new baby, I was exhausted. No matter what project I worked on, the managers found fault with it. Anthony grew more and more distant during that time and started spending a lot more time at his parents' house. I got fed up and told him it was time to choose between me or them. He made his choice. To be very honest, by that point I wasn't all that disappointed. I figured I'd just stay at the house for as long as I could with the baby or move back closer to my own folks because they offered to help watch her.

"Anthony moved back in with his parents and we filed for divorce, but we still worked together, which was very uncomfortable. We worked in teams that competed against each other on designs. Fortunately, we were assigned to different teams. It was awkward, but manageable, and I just tried to focus on my job. Still, I could sense that he didn't like me being there. A few weeks later, one of the engineers, a guy on my own design team named Chester Millfield, invited me out for a drink after work. Believe me, it wasn't a date or anything like that. You'd have to meet Chester to understand what I mean. I went out with him because he seemed genuinely sympathetic and I thought maybe he could offer some suggestions on how to make the situation better. We went to a local bar and I had two beers."

Amber paused and rubbed her hand through her hair. "I swear to you on my daughter's life that's all I had," she said as she fought back tears.

Katie reached over and touched her hand. "It's okay, Amber. Tell us what happened."

"When I came to I was strapped to a stretcher in an ambulance outside of some motel near the bar."

"Where was this Chester Millfield?" Katie asked.

"Gone. The police said they received an anonymous phone call about a woman doing drugs in the motel, and they found a needle with traces of heroin on the bed next to me. I was arrested for possession of a controlled substance in the ambulance on the way to the hospital. I swear to God I don't know how it got there."

"Did you tell them that you had been out with this Chester Millfield?"

"I did, and the police actually talked to him, but all he said was that he left me at my car and then he went to a friend's house afterwards to watch a game on TV."

"Do you know if they ever followed up on that? Investigated it, I mean?"

"They did, but the friend whose house he went to afterwards was Anthony's, and Anthony agreed with everything he said."

"Had you ever been arrested before?" Katie asked.

"Once, for possession of pot in college along with about twenty other kids. That's it."

Katie nodded for her to continue.

"Of course word of the arrest spread. I was terminated the next day."

"Without it even going to trial?" Katie asked surprised.

"Yes. Unbeknownst to me, there was a clause in my contract that said being arrested was grounds for termination because it made you a liability to the company. The work we do is so competitive, they were afraid of someone being bribed by a competitor."

"I don't think that's legal without an actual conviction," Katie observed. "It flies against the 'innocent until proven guilty' theory."

"Well, they got away with it. Anthony's attorney used the whole situation against me in court, said I was an 'unfit mother,' and the judge awarded Anthony full custody of our daughter. He also awarded him the house."

Amber started to cry. Katie brought out the tissue box.

"Thank you," she said as she gently blew her nose. "I'm so sorry. The thing is, I only get to see my daughter on the weekends now," she started to say but broke down again. Katie glanced over at Alexandria, who sat in the chair showing no emotion whatsoever.

"What was the disposition on the arrest, Amber?" Katie asked gently.

Amber pulled herself together. "They gave me a suspended sentence and sent me to counseling with a bunch of drug addicts."

"And when you were arrested and you told them about this Chester Millfield, did you tell the police that you thought you'd been set up?"

"I did, but it didn't matter."

"Why not?" Katie asked.

"Because they said I had drugs in my system when they arrested me."

Katie glanced over at Alexandria, who raised her eyebrow.

"You've got to believe me, I don't do drugs," she said with begging eyes.

UNBEKNOWNST TO AMBER GORDON, the chair she was sitting on was recording her pulse and blood pressure as she spoke. This data was being fed remotely to a computerized polygraph program in

43

the cybercision center that gauged the likelihood of someone telling the truth. That information was then fed back to Alexandria as she tapped on her laptop. Alexandria looked up and nodded ever so slightly to Katie.

Katie touched her knee. "It's okay, Amber, we believe you."

Amber Gordon dabbed at her eyes and her nose. "I just want my little girl back. That's all I want. I'll give up everything else, but I won't give her up. I can't. The only thing is…I don't have much money to pay you," she said.

"Don't worry about that right now, Amber," Katie said. "We work on a sliding fee scale. If we decide to take the case on, we can be flexible."

"Most of my money was spent on attorneys' fees. I hocked everything I owned for that. My parents even took out a second mortgage on their house to help me out. Right now I'm living in a subsidized housing project and trying to find work. I've applied to every engineering firm in the Northeast, but with the conviction on my record, no one will even respond to my letters and I don't want to move away from my daughter."

"What happened to Anthony?"

"He's still living in my—in our house—and he's hired a nanny to watch our daughter. Some stranger is raising my daughter…"

She broke down again and Katie waited patiently for her to recover.

"I can deal with being set up and the arrest, but I can't deal with not having my little girl," Amber said desperately.

"What's her name?" Katie asked.

"Vanessa. Vanessa Sumner."

Katie looked at her.

"You mean…?"

"Yes. My ex-husband is Anthony Sumner, the son of Donald Sumner, the president of Sumner Design."

KATIE SAT IN HER chair and swirled the scotch around the bottom of the glass while Margo took the old flowers, which, to Katie's eye, still looked fresh, out of the vase and replaced them with new ones.

"So we have a very unusual situation," Katie explained to them all. Jane sat across from Alexandria and took notes on a pad while Alexandria stroked Divinity. Divinity began to crawl up Alexandria's left arm. Jane, who was sitting to Alexandria's left, shifted as far back in her seat as possible. Alexandria shifted closer to Jane.

"We have a woman who's been sexually harassed by her own father-in-law's company; has possibly been set up for a false arrest by her husband; lost her career, her home, and worst of all, her daughter."

"So much for four billion years of evolution," Margo said as she trimmed the stem of the blue hyacinth to fit it in the vase. "Believe me, there ain't nothin' like having your innocent ass pronounced guilty when you know you didn't do it. And believe me," she said, glancing at her behind, "I had plenty for a conviction."

"It sounds as if her biggest offense was trying to work and have a baby," Jane offered. "In this day and age, I find that incredible. Alice has managed very well with MaryJane," she added. "Just the other day she said…"

"Has any man yet asked another man for advice on how to combine a marriage and a career?" Katie said interrupting. "So, do we take the case?"

"I say we kick their sorry asses as far as we can," Margo said.

"Are we solvent enough to do some gratis work, Janie?" Katie asked. "Janie?"

"Oh, sorry," Jane said as she watched Divinity out of the corner of her eye. "Financially we can afford a gratis case, but I wouldn't recommend we make a habit of it."

"Alex?"

Alexandria sat up quickly, which set Divinity in a race down her leg, headed right toward Jane. Jane tucked her legs in and squeezed into the corner of her chair.

"For God's sake, Alex, would you put that thing away!" Katie said.

Alex scooped Divinity back up in her hand and began stroking her back.

"Yes."

"All right then, it's settled. Alex, I want you to start digging up everything you can on this Chester Millfield who took Amber out that night. Find out who he is, what his interests are—you know, the full background. Janie, I want you to take a good look at Sumner Design. Go over their financials and tell me if there's anything hinky about the way they do business. Margo, I want you to look into the Sumner family. Find out who they are, any skeletons in the closet, that kind of thing. The only way we're going to get Amber Gordon her daughter back," Katie said as she reached for one of their trademark chocolate spiders, "is if we can prove that she was set up."

"And how exactly are we going to do that, Oh White Wonder?" Margo asked.

Katie held the chocolate spider in front of her and twisted it around in the air. "By thinking like one of these," she said as she popped it into her mouth. "The black widow spins her nest, then waits for her prey to come to her." She stood up and put on her coat.

"Where are you going?" Alexandria asked.

"To the Bitches and Stitches Club."

"Pass me the skein, dear," Molly Mahoney said. Katie picked up the skein of pink yarn and passed it to her mother. Her mother's red hair had faded to gray years ago, but she still wore it long and pulled back in a bun. Another woman passed by their chairs and admired Molly Mahoney's knitting.

"Looks good, Molly. Is that for your girl?"

"It is," Molly said very loudly. "But not this one, Peggy," she said as she nodded her head toward Katie. "Peggy, this is my daughter, Katie. Katie, this is Mrs. McAfee. Her husband, Pete, was on the job in the East Division."

"Hello," Katie said loudly.

"Mrs. McAfee got the very last room here, so we're helping her get settled in."

The woman nodded and settled down in a chair across the open room and took out a bag of cross-stitch projects.

Katie looked around the recreation room of Shamrock Shores, the brand-new assisted living facility her mother was now living in. Not that her mother needed much in the way of assistance, but it gave Katie peace of mind to know that her mother was not alone. The units had filled quickly, which amazed Katie considering how expensive they were. The monthly cost for her mother's small condo was almost as much as Katie was paying for her own modest apartment. Her parents' home of nearly forty years had been sold for an outrageous price, the money carefully placed in an interest-bearing account, and yet, depending on how long her mother lived, it still might not be enough.

"How's the food been, Mom?" Katie asked. Though they each had their own kitchens, there was also a community cafeteria that specialized in what Katie called "Old Fogey Food," consisting of high fiber this and soft that.

"The food is fine, dear," her mother began. Then she leaned forward and said very quietly, "Some of us have been sneaking into Annie Timmons' room at night. She's got a stockpot. Cooks a fine pot roast in it. Lots of red wine in the sauce and a bit out of it, too."

Katie smiled and reached next to her for the canvas bag she had brought, filled to the top with skeins of yarn.

"Which reminds me, here's the yarn you asked me to get," Katie said, winking. Molly Mahoney set her knitting down, looked around carefully to make sure no one was watching and gently lifted the skeins of yarn aside to see the bottles of Jack Daniels hidden beneath, protected from rattling by more skeins of yarn shoved in between.

"Is that the right color?" Katie asked smiling.

"Perfect," her mother said as she winked back at her daughter. Then she leaned forward and whispered, "Jesus, Mary, and Joseph, if I'd known about that rule before, I would have told you you'd have to bring me here over my dead body."

"It's for all the residents on medication, Mom. They're not supposed to mix booze and meds."

Her mother waved her off and pointed her finger at Katie. "When you get to my age, it's your own damn business what you do with your life."

Molly Mahoney lifted her arm up to reset her work in progress and slapped at the loose skin underneath her arms. "Look at that, Katie," she said. "You reach my age and you look like you've got flying squirrels hanging off your arms."

"Oh Ma, you look fine," Katie assured her.

"You wait, Katie. I have more red and blue lines on my legs than a Rand McNally map."

Molly Mahoney looked across the room and met the smile of a gray-haired man sitting in his chair reading the paper. Katie watched as her mother shifted slightly in her chair and sat up a little more. The gray-haired man nodded toward Katie.

"Who's that, Mom?" Katie asked quietly.

Her mother quickly picked up her knitting again. "Oh, that's Mr. Timothy Collins," she said nonchalantly, but Katie could see a slight rise of color in her mother's pale Irish skin. "He's retired from the State. He met your father a few times. Very nice gentleman."

Katie looked over and met the man's glance. He smiled at Katie again and looked back down at his paper.

"He seems quite smitten," Katie said.

"Oh, Katie Mahoney," her mother said, blushing, "the things you imagine. He's as deaf as a tree."

"Are you planning on slipping into his room at night, too?" Katie asked mischievously.

"Kathleen Ann," her mother said sternly, but then she smiled.

Molly took the canvas bag from Katie and set it down very carefully next to her. Then she reached into her own bag.

"Oh, before I forget, I have something for you," she said as she took out a folded green flyer. "Shamrock Shores is having their grand opening celebration in a few weeks. I thought perhaps you and Kelly might want to come."

"I don't know, Mom," Katie said, interrupting her. "With my crazy work schedule and all…"

"Katie," her mother said, peering over her glasses, "she's your sister."

"I know, Mom, but she's busy, too. She's got all those bad guys to defend."

"Katie, you do your work and she does hers. I wish you would stop treating her like she's the enemy."

"I didn't say she was the enemy, Mom, but you can't ask a cop to respect someone who defends criminals for a living. You know what they say, Mom, ninety-nine percent of the lawyers give the rest a bad name."

"Your father the cop respected her, Katie. He said we all have a job to do. He was proud of both of you, may he rest in peace and the Good Lord watch over him."

Katie shoved the paper into her bag. She passed her mother another skein of yarn. Molly took off her glasses. She only needed them for close-up work since her eyes were still very sharp, along with everything else. Now she reached over and lifted her daughter's chin up, just as she'd been doing since she was a small child.

"It's not really about her choice in jobs, is it, Katie?"

Katie said nothing. Molly Mahoney dropped her hand and said, "I heard Joe made captain recently."

Katie nodded, but quietly slipped her hand into her pocket.

"If you see him, tell him I said 'congratulations,' would you?"

Katie looked at her mother like she had lost her mind.

"Oh, come on now, Katie," her mother said, "things aren't always what they seem." Katie ignored her.

Defeated, Molly asked, "And how is business?"

"Busy. Very busy."

"How are the other Spider Women?"

"Black Widows, Ma, and they're all fine."

"Does that tall girl still have that spider?"

"The tarantula? Yes."

"She's a wee odd, don't you think?"

"She just does her own thing."

"I worry about you, Katie."

"Don't worry about me, Ma."

"But you're all alone."

"Not really, Ma. We all look out for each other."

"But you said yourself, you barely know that one with the spider."

"It doesn't matter, Ma. Sometimes you don't need to know every single detail about a person to know they'll watch out for you."

"Katie, the Good Lord doesn't want us to live our lives with hatred and bitterness…"

"Ma, please."

Her mother studied her for a minute, then put her glasses back on. Just then, Katie's cell phone began beeping. With much relief, she withdrew it from her pocket. Keeping the screen from her mother's view, she flipped it open. The words "rescue page" appeared on the screen and Katie knew Alexandria had sent them.

"I'm sorry, Ma, but I have to take off," Katie said as she bent over and gave her mother a kiss on the cheek. "I'll stop by next week."

"Katie, go see your sister, would you?"

"I will, Ma."

"And Father Flaherty says he hasn't seen you at mass in ages..."

KATIE WATCHED AS ALEXANDRIA brought up an aerial photo on the big screen and zoomed down into an industrial park. She drew a square around several buildings.

"This is Sumner Design," Alexandria explained, "located in the industrial park on the West side."

"Doesn't look like much," Margo observed.

"It's not supposed to," Alex explained. "They like to keep things low key because of the competitive nature of the business."

Jane looked away from Divinity for just a second to ask, "What is that thing moving on the screen?"

"That's a person," Alexandria explained. "We're watching a live satellite feed."

Jane nodded, then glanced back down at Divinity as she fanned herself.

"Sumner Design," Alexandria went on, "is solely focused on designing car parts for the automotive industry. Those parts are then brokered out to automotive manufacturers, parts stores, etc."

"Financials?" Katie asked, looking at Jane, who was watching Divinity. "Janie?"

"Sorry," Jane said, gathering herself. "Sumner Design has been in business for thirty-two years. They are privately owned and did well up until the late nineties, but their cash flow has dwindled over the last five years since investing in a brand-new manufacturing plant that was supposed to be state-of-the-art."

"What happened?" Katie asked.

"From the article I read, the software didn't work as promised."

Alexandria chimed in. "They went with first versions, beta stuff, which is a no-no. They should have held off for another year until the software developer got it right."

"In any case," Jane continued, "it took them two years to get the plant off the ground and by then it had cost them millions in losses. They've yet to recover."

"So where do they stand now?"

"Seeking venture capital to pull them back out of the hole."

"Really…" Katie said thinking, "and if they don't find a VC angel to sit on their shoulders?"

"I don't see how they could last much longer. Their cash flow is dwindling and sales are down," Jane said.

Katie sipped her drink as she mulled this over.

MARGO NODDED TO ALEXANDRIA and a picture of a middle-aged woman in a beige suit appeared. She was standing next to several other people at a ribbon-cutting ceremony for a day care center. In her hands, she clutched a pair of over-sized scissors and was smiling directly into the camera.

"This is Edwina Sumner," Margo began, "the fifty-eight-year-old wife of Donald Sumner, president of Sumner Design. She's into charity events, nonprofits, ribbon cuttings, and all that stuff you rich white women do."

"Who you calling a rich white woman?" Katie asked.

"Well, if you ask me," Margo answered, "that woman looks like she could scare the flies off a pile of shit. Sorry, Jane. Anyway, I wouldn't want to be messing with her."

"Sumner Design contributes a fair amount to nonprofits and charitable organizations, especially of late," Jane added.

Katie looked at Jane with raised eyebrows.

"How can they afford to do that if they're going down the tubes?" she asked.

"They can't afford much, but they do need a certain amount of tax write-offs, and donations are the easiest ones to get. They're also probably hoping to give the impression to potential venture capitalists that they're more solvent than they actually are," Jane explained.

Katie nodded. "Any skeletons? Lovers?"

"None that I could find."

Margo nodded to Alexandria again and a new photo appeared of two men, one with dark hair, one with silver hair, sitting on the deck of a large white sailboat.

"This is Anthony and his father, Donald Sumner, aboard their boat, *Sumner Fun*," Margo explained, rolling her eyes. "Soon after the divorce, Anthony hired a young, live-in au pair to care for the little girl."

"Let's hope the au pair is at least very loving," Jane stated.

"Oh, she's very loving all right. Rumor has it this girl's like a doorknob."

"Huh?" Jane asked.

"Everybody gets a turn."

Jane blushed, shook her head, and said, "I don't understand— if this was Amber's own father-in-law's company, how could they treat her so poorly?"

"Because," Katie explained, "the father-in-law obviously doesn't give a sh—" she caught herself. "…hoot about how women are treated. That kind of corporate sexual harassment happens all across the country every single day. Why do you think they hired mostly single mothers? Because they're the most vulnerable, the ones with the most to lose, who rely on every nickel and dime to get by to support their kids. When Amber complained, she put the company in jeopardy of being exposed. This creep, Anthony, only cares about being able to inherit the family business and doesn't give a flying f—" she stopped and glanced toward Jane. "…doesn't give a blessed cow about anyone but himself. He must have figured once they had the baby she'd be a 'good girl' and stay home. When she announced she was coming back, they needed to get rid of her, yet they couldn't just fire her. So they set her up."

"How awful," Jane said.

"Rat-ass bastards," Margo said, then, "Sorry, Jane."

"Do we have the medical report from the night of the arrest?" Katie asked. Alexandria tapped her keyboard and zoomed in on the report.

Jane stiffened in her chair. "I thought medical records were private."

Katie glanced at Alexandria before saying, "It's okay, Janie, she signed a release."

Jane nodded but watched nervously as Divinity changed direction and started crawling down Alexandria's leg toward her.

Katie read the on-screen report for quite some time. "Wait a second," she said as she had Alexandria flip back and forth page by page. She sat back in her chair.

"Idiots," she said under her breath.

Margo and Jane looked at each other. "Who's an idiot?" Margo asked.

"Whoever investigated her case. Her blood work showed the presence of substantial amounts of GHB."

"What is that, Katie?" Jane asked.

"Gamma hydroxybutyrate, commonly known as 'GHB' or the date rape drug. It's also called Serenity or Paint Stripper or Liquid E and a bunch of other names. It's popular at rave parties and is distributed in powder, vial, or liquid form. As a liquid, it's odorless and tasteless."

"You mean that guy could have slipped it in her drink?"

"Easily, without her knowing it."

Alexandria pulled up the arrest report. Katie studied it with equal interest.

"For God's sakes," she said.

"What is it, Katie?" Jane asked.

"The only needle mark they found on her was in-between her toes, a common place for addicts to shoot up."

"So?" Margo asked.

Katie looked at her. "It's awfully hard to shoot yourself up with a needle between the toes when you're unconscious."

Margo held her hand up. "Now don't say I didn't warn you, but the next photo you're about to see is so damn ugly, it could make an onion cry," she added as she nodded to Alexandria.

A picture of an extremely obese man popped up on screen.

"This big boy is Chester Millfield, the guy who Amber thinks set her up that night." Margo turned to Katie and said, "And you say African-American names are strange?"

"Keep going, Taneesha," Katie said.

Margo smiled. "It turns out Chester has a few skeletons in his closet."

"Skeletons?" Katie said, looking at the picture. "Isn't that an oxymoron?"

"Or maybe just a 'moron'," Margo added, laughing.

Jane frowned and shook her head.

"Anyway," Margo said, clearing her throat, "it seems that this dude, Chester, has been picked up a few times for engaging the company of certain…for-profit ladies. He likes going to the hardware store."

"I beg your pardon?" Jane asked.

"Twenty-five cents a screw."

"Like he's going to get it for free?" Katie added. "Sorry, Janie."

"Last time I saw something that ugly, I pinned a tail on it," Margo continued. "This boy's so big he's making me look like a flagpole. Anyway, he can't bring them home because he still lives with his momma."

"Oh no!" Katie said. "Not a momma's boy!" She and Margo groaned.

Jane frowned and let out a huge sigh. They shut up. "I'll remind you that obesity is considered a disease," Jane said as she vigorously applied a damp cloth against her neck.

Margo looked down at her own ample figure and said, "Do I look like I have any damn disease? The only thing I'm suffering from is liking my own damn cooking too much."

Katie cleared her throat and in a business-like tone said, "Janie's right. Can I get you something cool to drink, Janie?"

Jane declined.

"How come Chester got arrested, but hasn't gotten fired?" Alexandria chimed in.

"My thoughts exactly," Katie said. "A double standard, for sure. Margo, I want you and Alex to dig deeper into this Chester Millfield." And because she couldn't resist, she added, "He could be hiding something right under our noses and we'd never even see it." She and Margo burst out laughing.

"I have work to do," Jane said coolly as she walked out.

"Aw, come on, Janie," Katie said.

"What's her damn problem?" Margo asked.

"You know how she is," Katie said as she got up.

"Are you going to talk to her?"

"Not now," Katie said slightly annoyed. "She's too irritable right now. Better to let her cool down, literally and figuratively. Besides, she'll forget about it in a little while," Katie said as she grabbed her jacket.

"So where are you going, girl?"

"I'm going to that bar that Amber and Chester went to that night to see if anyone remembers anything."

"You really think someone's gonna remember something that happened nine months ago?" Margo asked skeptically.

Katie gestured back at the screen displaying Chester's picture.

"Would you forget that?" she asked.

"I'd sure as hell try to," Margo said, smirking.

6

Katie arrived at Sam's Saloon just as it opened. A waitress was still turning all the chairs upright. The room was very dark and Katie paused in the doorway for a few seconds to allow her eyes to adjust. She strode up to the bar, reached into her pocket, took out a wallet, and quickly flashed a badge, one of many that she kept stashed in her drawer back at the office.

"Liquor Commission," she announced to the young bartender.

He looked up nervously at her.

"I'm here to investigate an incident about nine months ago involving a woman who may have been served while intoxicated," she began.

It was the worst charge she could think of. No legitimate drinking establishment wanted to risk losing their license for overserving.

"Do you remember this woman?" Katie asked taking out a photo of Amber Gordon from her pocket.

"No, but I…"

"What about this man?" Katie asked cutting him off. It was a tactic she had learned during interrogations.

"No, but I…"

"Look, my report can go either way depending on how much cooperation I get here," she warned sternly.

"But I've only worked here for a month," he finally blurted out.

Disappointed, she looked around. "What about her?" she asked pointing to the waitress.

He shrugged.

"Excuse me," Katie said, flashing the badge again. "Liquor Commission," she announced. "I'm investigating a possible over-serving of an intoxicated subject," she said.

The woman with bleached-blonde hair eyed her suspiciously.

"I've never seen you in here before," she said.

"Bobby O'Leary's tied up on a big case," she said, praying the name was still good. "I'm covering some of his territory," she added.

The woman nodded.

"Do you remember ever seeing this woman in here?" she asked, pulling Amber's picture out.

The blonde looked at it for a few moments. "I'm not sure. Maybe," she said.

"What about this guy?" Katie asked as she pulled Chester's picture out. The recognition was instant.

"Oh yeah, he's in here a lot. Hard to miss him, if you know what I mean."

"Do you remember ever seeing them together in here?" she asked.

The woman eyed Katie.

"Look, if everyone cooperates, my report can be very neutral, if you get where I'm going. I'm not looking to put anyone out of business here. I just want to know the truth."

"Maybe I remember them here one night."

"Maybe you can tell me about that."

"Maybe I can."

Katie and the waitress sat down across from each other.

"He usually comes in alone, so I remember it was strange that he had the girl with him that night, especially since she was pretty and he's so... You know what I'm saying."

"Yeah, a face every mother but his would like to forget," Katie said.

"Exactly. So this one night he brings the girl in. She seemed nice. I think maybe they work together or something. Don't quote me on that, but I think I heard them say something about a project."

Katie nodded and let her go on.

"She was sober when they got here, that I'm sure of. I've been in this business for fifteen years and believe me, I know when someone's tanked. She wasn't when she came in."

"What did she order?"

"She had two beers."

"You're sure about that?"

"Absolutely. I remember everyone by their drinks."

"So what kind of shape was she in when she left?" Katie saw the hesitation. "Look," she said, "I'm going to be completely honest with you because you look like a hard-working lady and I don't want to waste any more of your time than I need to. I think you know something and that's why you remember this situation. So how about you just tell me everything you remember and then I'll get the hell out of your hair?"

"She was sober when she came in, but she sure as hell was high when she left. She was slurring her words and swaying and he had to practically carry her out the door."

"What do you think happened?"

The woman looked around the room. "Look, this is a legitimate business," she said.

"Understood, and again, my report is wide open right now. What do you think happened?"

"If I had seen her go to the ladies room, I would say maybe she juiced up in there, but she didn't. I know because I was watching her. She stayed at the table the whole time."

"You think maybe someone slipped something in her beer?" Katie asked.

The woman shrugged. "Probably. I've seen it before."

"Did anyone ever stop by afterward, the police I mean, and ask you anything about this?"

"No."

Katie shook her head. "Thank you," she said, rising. "I don't think there'll be any problem with the report based on the information you gave me, but I'm going to have to ask you to keep this all very quiet until the investigation is complete."

"Are you kidding me?" the woman said. "I don't need any trouble from the Liquor Commission. I'm Sam and I own the damn place."

"ANY LUCK ON THE bar?" Margo asked Katie when she returned.

"Sorry to say," Katie began, "that my brothers in blue never bothered to check Amber's story with the bar owner or maybe they would have realized she was telling the truth."

"So what do we do now?" Margo asked.

"The black widow spider," Katie began, "hangs belly upward waiting for her prey to get trapped in her web."

Margo looked at her with a quizzical expression on her face.

"You white girls sure do talk funny sometimes. Now how about you put that in damn English for me?"

"Meaning we start spinning webs to see just who gets trapped." Katie reached for her cell phone and glanced back at her notes.

"Who are you calling?" Margo asked.

"The prey," Katie said, covering the mouthpiece with her hand. "Yes, good afternoon. I'd like to speak with Mr. Donald Sumner, please. Kathleen Kennedy of Angel Capital calling. Thank you, I'll hold…"

KATIE SAT IN THE driver's seat of the parked white van with the "Divinity Digital Products" logo temporarily painted on its side and looked over at the entrance of Sumner Design. Hidden in the dots of the "i's" on the logo were several tiny cameras recording details of the building in case they needed to made a covert entry.

Katie turned away as a pedestrian walked by. Empty boxes sat on the seat next to her. She waited patiently.

"You sure you trust her to do this?" Alexandria asked from the back as she glanced at the laptop resting on a shelf in front of her.

"She'll be fine. All she has to do is make the delivery," Katie said.

"She's not exactly undercover material," Alexandria said.

"And you are?" Katie asked in a slightly annoyed tone. "Look, she's going through a tough time right now with this menopause thing. It's good for her to get out of the office and see the other side of the operations. That way she'll feel like she's a part of the team and get her mind off her body. She was very excited when I asked her."

Alexandria turned to the monitor. "I'm starting to get something."

They were "war driving"—sniffing out wireless computer traffic as the data traveled through the air.

Alexandria tapped a few more keys. "They're operating at a fairly high level of encryption on a virtual private network."

"Can you penetrate it?"

"No."

"No?" Katie asked as she swiveled around to face her. "You can't penetrate their network?"

"I didn't say that. I said I can't penetrate the encrypted part, however…" Her hands flew furiously over the keyboards as she watched the two mounted monitors.

Katie saw the slight smile cross her lips. She looked up at Katie.

"Bingo," she said.

"Okay, Goddess of the Geeks, explain…"

"After the Black Widow snags its prey in its web, it makes small punctures in the victim's body and then it sucks the liquid contents out of it."

"You do realize you're starting to sound like me. And thanks for that visual," Katie said dryly, "but what does it mean?"

"It means I've just made a small puncture wound in their network. When we get back to the cybercision center, I'll start sucking the data out of it. Their network was buttoned down very tight."

"Except—" Katie said.

"…except they forgot to lock down the security on one of their fax machines that has a wireless network card installed in it. I've grabbed the IP address off of that machine and will spoof it with a backdoor penetration. I've already installed a rootkit on one of their computers so I can penetrate it again when we get back to the office," Alexandria said with a sly grin.

"You really get off on this stuff, don't you? You want to smoke a cigarette or something after all this digital penetration?" Katie teased.

KATIE TURNED TO THE monitor, which showed Jane's view from the buttonhole cameras attached to her shirt, hat, and clipboard. The screen showed a young woman flipping through a folder, shaking her head.

Katie turned the volume up.

"And you're sure they're ours?" the woman asked. "Because I don't have anything listed in my order book."

"Look," Katie heard Jane say just as they had rehearsed, "I've got about a thousand of these in my van and to be honest, I don't feel like going back and forth because I'm old and tired, so why don't you just save us both the headache and keep them. Let the main office figure out who messed up the order."

A FEW MOMENTS LATER, Jane emerged from the building empty-handed.

"Oh dear heavens," Jane said, waving her hand at her face. "I've never been so nervous in my entire life."

Katie reached over and patted Jane's knee. "You did great, Janie. You're a regular Charlie's Angel. When they install their new car-shaped computer mice, we'll have an even better look-see at what goes on at Sumner Design from all the cameras and microphones embedded in them."

"I was so afraid that something would fall off, or that they'd somehow see the cameras," Jane said as she fanned herself. She was very breathless.

"You okay, Janie?" Katie asked.

"My goodness. I think I'm having a major hot flash."

Katie glanced in the rearview mirror and caught Alexandria rolling her eyes.

"In that case," Katie said, "as soon as I'm done, we'll get you something cool to drink," she said as she opened the van door and stepped out.

KATIE SMOOTHED HER VERY tight skirt back down and pulled open the heavy glass door. Inside the entrance of Sumner Design was a small reception desk and behind it, a long series of cubicles where she could hear laughter rising.

"May I help you?" a young, red-headed woman asked.

"Kathleen Kennedy of Angel Capital to see Mr. Donald Sumner," she said in a brisk, business-like tone. She brought her leather briefcase, with its hidden camera in the handle, up to the counter and set it down.

"I'm sorry, Miss…"

"Kennedy," Katie offered.

"I'm sorry, Miss Kennedy, but I don't see the appointment on his schedule."

Katie suddenly realized that several men, including the rather obese Chester Millfield, had risen from their cubicles and were eyeing her. A few drifted toward each other, gave each other nudges ,and nodded her way. Katie shifted her position. "There must be a mistake," she said. "I made the appointment last week."

The young woman shook her head and looked at the monitor. "I'm very sorry, but I don't have anything on his calendar," she said again.

Just then, Katie felt a presence behind her. She turned to see an attractive young man, whom she immediately recognized as Anthony Sumner, standing there. He very casually leaned on the counter and Katie watched as his eyes drifted down to the deep cut in her sweater.

"It's all right, Doreen," he said. "My father is expecting Miss Kennedy," he said as he offered his hand. Katie watched his eyes travel up and down her as she shook his hand. "I'm Donald Sumner's son, Anthony," he said smiling. Katie smiled and deliberately flicked her hair back.

"Katie," she said as he held onto her hand a little too long.

Doreen slid a visitor's guestbook over and asked her to sign in. She deliberately signed "K-A-T-I" in lower case and drew an annoying little heart over the "i." Anthony Sumner watched her and smiled. Katie tossed her hair back again.

"Very well, let me show you to Mr. Sumner's office," Doreen began to say, but Anthony waved her off with his hand. "No need,

Doreen," he said. "I'll show Miss Kennedy." Doreen gave him an annoyed look and sat back down.

Before they were out of earshot, Anthony Sumner said, "Don't mind her, she probably messed up the appointment."

"Father," Anthony began as if he had just landed a prized trout, "this is Miss Katie Kennedy from Angel Capital," he explained.

"Well, hello," Donald Sumner said, as he immediately rose and came around from his massive mahogany desk. Like son, like father, Katie watched as Donald Sumner's eyes went up and down her body and momentarily fixed on the deep V of her sweater. "The pleasure is mine," he said smoothly as he took her hand and, without any warning, kissed the back of it.

Not a hair was out of place on his silver head. He was deeply tanned and had the relaxed look of a man who had had an easy life. He gestured to a leather couch upon which Katie sat gingerly, fully aware her skirt was so short she was near to indecent. Donald Sumner's eyes drifted down her legs to the high heels. He turned back to his son.

"Thank you, Anthony," he said.

Father and son exchanged looks. "I thought perhaps I could sit in on the meeting," Anthony Sumner began but his father quickly cut him off.

"No need for that," he said. "Besides, you need to get back to your team." Anthony Sumner cast his father an angry glance before turning around and reluctantly walking out.

"Now, Miss Kennedy…"

"Katie, please," she said.

"Very well, Katie, I understand you are here on some mutually interesting business." He turned and strode over to a cherry cabinet to reveal a wet bar. "May I offer you a drink?"

"Perhaps just a splash of scotch," Katie said. "Neat. Just a little," Katie added as she watched Donald Sumner pour them both an ample glassful. The rich taste of the scotch slid smoothly down the back of her throat. Katie held up the glass and examined it. Donald Sumner watched her carefully.

"Excellent," Katie said.

"That's ten-year-old Glenmarngie," Donald Sumner explained. He peered at her over his glass. "I can't imagine waiting ten years for something that gives one so much pleasure."

Katie peered back at him and gave a coquettish grin. "Nor can I," she said.

Donald Sumner smiled at her.

Katie set her glass down on a nearby side table. "As I explained to you earlier on the phone, Mr. Sumner…"

"Donald, please."

"Very well, Donald, as I explained to you earlier on the phone, I represent a number of individuals interested in investment opportunities with established companies. The whole dot.com fiasco has made many of these investors gun-shy of start-ups. They're no longer willing to land on the shoulders of a company that does not have an established history."

"A wise decision," Donald Sumner said, placing his hand lightly on her knee. "In this day and age, one has to be very particular whom one chooses to have a relationship with," he said.

Katie let her eyes linger on him for a moment and made no effort to move his hand away.

"Nicely put," she said in an encouraging tone. Donald Sumner smiled. "In any case, the clients I represent understand that you are seeking venture capital financing on a short-term basis."

Donald Sumner slowly withdrew his hand from her knee. "May I ask who these clients you represent are?" he said.

Katie shook her head. "Discreet ones, Donald. They've made their fortunes mostly in the high-tech arena but are smart enough to diversify their portfolios."

"And what is your role in all of this?"

"I'm like a scouting agent looking for companies that need a moderate infusion of cash, but also appear to have a solid track record."

"Like a trading scout in sports?"

"Yes."

"Do you like sports, Katie?" The hand suddenly reappeared on her knee.

"As a matter of fact, I do," she said, batting her eyes and leaning over. She returned the favor by placing her hand on his knee. His eyes traveled back down to her sweater and he shifted in his seat a little closer.

"How lucky am I?" he asked her.

"Time will tell," Katie said smiling. She removed her hand and said, "As I indicated to you on the phone, I'll need a full breakdown of your financials, APs, ARs, P&L's, holdings, etc., to bring back to my clients."

"I have an idea," Donald Sumner began. "Why don't I take you to dinner tonight and we can go over all of that."

Katie looked as regretful as she could. "Unfortunately, I need to be on a plane to Chicago tonight, but I will be back in town very soon," she said. "In the meantime, if you could just e-mail me everything I've requested." She handed him a silver business card with "Angel Capital" imprinted on it along with a phony P.O. box and a phone number that would be answered back at the office with the correct name. Alexandria had already created a website and history of Angel Capital on the Internet, including several false press releases and news write-ups.

Donald looked genuinely disappointed. "Perhaps another time, then," he offered.

"We will meet again, Donald," Katie said. "That I can assure you."

She rose and Donald placed a firm hand on her back which quickly slipped downward. He escorted her to the door. As they paused, Donald took her hand in his, leaned forward, and kissed it, while saying, "The pleasure has been mine."

As Katie walked out of Donald Sumner's office, she saw an even larger crowd of men standing around their cubicles. She was aware of all their eyes on her as she walked past the receptionist's desk. The young woman, Doreen, shrugged apologetically at her. Katie strutted out until she was all the way around the block. She banged twice on the back of the van's doors and climbed in. Alexandria gave Jane the signal to go and they drove off.

"They've already installed the mice," Alexandria said.

"Let's have a look-see," Katie said. Alexandria switched the monitor to the hidden camera view and turned up the volume. They both watched as a group of men stood around a cubicle, all displaying their "Sumner Design" ID tags.

"Great video quality," Katie noted.

"It ought to be, these are top-of-the line micro cameras," Alexandria explained.

"Turn it up."

"Sumner's such a lucky bastard," Chester Millfield said as he rolled up his sleeves. "Did you get a load of those tits?"

"I got a load all right," one of them said, rubbing at his crotch. "I bet Sumner did too," and they all laughed.

"Who was she?" one of them asked.

"I don't care who she was, I just hope she comes back," Chester Millfield said. "Maybe it's the old man's birthday or something."

"If it is, we should all get a piece of the cake."

Anthony Sumner drifted into the frame of the video. "What're you boys doing?" he asked casually.

"Trying to recover from the boobshell that just came in to visit your old man," one said.

"We noticed you didn't get invited to the meeting," Chester said.

"Doesn't matter," Anthony said. "She's a total airhead. Besides, I like mine thinner than that. Not as heavy a load in the back end," he added.

Katie's smug smile disappeared immediately. "That son of a bitch," she said. Alexandria said nothing.

"Who cares if the caboose is pulling a few extra cars along when it has headlights like that?" one of the men asked.

"Because you start pulling extra cars around for too long and the next thing you know there's extra cars everywhere and you won't even be able to find the headlights," Anthony Sumner explained. The men all laughed.

"Bastards!" Katie said. "Shut it off."

Alexandria flicked the monitor switch off. Katie stamped her foot on the floor of the van.

"Those assholes are going down."

8

ALEXANDRIA REACHED INTO THE small screened box and pulled out a cricket. It kicked its legs furiously as it tried to escape her grip. She then opened the top of the glass aquarium and dropped the cricket in. The cricket scrambled to the side of the glass but she placed the cover back on quickly, preventing its escape. Alexandria watched intently as Divinity sensed the small insect's vibrations and slowly wandered out of her corner. The cricket made several futile attempts at escaping. With lightning speed, Divinity struck and easily overpowered her prey. Satisfied, Alexandria walked back into the conference room.

MARGO PASSED THE PLATTER around the room.

"What are these, Sister?" Marcus asked, admiring the delicacies.

"Asparagus wraps," Margo explained. "They're baked in a fillo dough with a little soft cheese."

"And these?" Antoine asked.

"Petit quiche with salmon and red peppers," Margo said. "As always, there are no calories."

"No thanks," Katie said as Margo passed the platter. Everyone looked at her.

"They're really good, Katie," Jane said. "You should try one."

"I'm sure they are."

"What's wrong, Katarina?" Marcus said, "Having a bout of anorexia or something?"

"I'm fine. I'm just not hungry." They all looked at her incredulously because Katie had an iron stomach and could out-eat any of them. They politely said nothing. Katie looked at Alexandria but knew she wouldn't say anything about the comment Andrew Sumner had made about her "caboose."

"I can only imagine," Jane said lightly to Marcus, "what your sister must have been whipping up in her EZ Bake oven as a little girl."

Margo gave her brother a push on the shoulder.

"Ow!" Marcus said, rubbing his arm.

"Go ahead, Marcus, tell them."

"I don't know what you're talking about," Marcus said as he waved her off and brushed his silk pants.

Margo ignored him and told the story herself. "Marcus got extremely jealous of the fact that I got the Barbie Goes to Hawaii doll and he didn't, so he took the chemistry set that he didn't want and concocted the most foul-smelling experiment he could possibly put together and baked it in my EZ Bake Oven. Momma had to throw the whole damn thing out, it stunk so bad."

"It wasn't fair," Marcus protested, peering over his glass, "that I got the G.I. Joe, the pseudo-machismo iconoclastic affirmation for every heterosexual young male…although I did like the fact that he was wearing a uniform, though whatever bitch came up with the concept of 'gunmetal gray' ought to be shot."

"So instead, he dressed his G.I. Joe in my Barbie wedding gown," Margo added. They all laughed.

"Not exactly haute couture," Marcus added, "but it was the best I could do. Cheap sateen, even cheaper lace. What a travesty."

Just then, Marcus' cellphone began ringing.

"Speak to me, darling," he answered. "Oh dear," he said as he motioned for Antoine to come with him. They slipped out of the room.

"KEEP AN EYE OUT for the e-mail from Donald Sumner," Katie said to Margo. "Make sure you get it to Jane a.s.a.p. so she can see what they look like financially."

"You told me the same damn thing half an hour ago," Margo said.

Ignoring her, Katie turned to Alexandria and said, "He had a laptop on his desk that could be worth taking a look at if there's any way we can penetrate it."

"I tried. They're using a heavily encrypted firewall."

"Well, try again," she said with some sharpness in her tone. Alexandria glanced at her while Jane and Margo looked at each other, wondering why Katie was in such a foul mood. Katie got up and refilled her drink.

"I'll tell you one thing about the old man," Katie said, "he wasted no time making moves on me. When he asked me if I liked sports, I thought he was going to suggest we play ball right then and there. Asshole," she said as she, without thinking, popped an asparagus wrap in her mouth. "Can you imagine the audacity of those sons of…" She paused, realized she had put food in her mouth, and quickly spit it out in her napkin.

"What's wrong?" Margo asked. "Is it that bad?"

"No, it's just that I didn't mean to…I wasn't thinking, I just…" Katie glanced from Margo to Jane, then fixed on Alexandria, who remained expressionless. "Oh, go ahead. Tell them," she said finally.

"Tell them what?" Alexandria asked innocently.

"Just tell them," Katie ordered.

"By the time Katie got back out to the van," Alexandria began, "they had already installed the car mice and had a few unkind things to say about our esteemed leader."

"Such as?" Margo asked eyeing Katie cautiously.

"They said she had a few extra cars on her caboose," Alexandria said.

Margo bit her lip and tried not to smile. They all knew Katie could be incredibly vain about her body at times. She always told them how she used to run all the time because the stress of police work demanded top form. No one had seen her run in a while.

Katie scowled. "Bastards," she muttered again. "Sorry, Janie," she said as she stood up. "Do you see extra cars back there?" she asked pointing to her butt.

"You have a lovely body, Katie," Jane offered. "It's very feminine."

Katie rolled her eyes. "Oh brother," she said as she sat back down.

"Katie," Margo began, "my ass is so fat I could sell shade. I had my blood type tested the other day and you know what it came back as?"

"What?"

"Rocky road, so don't you be bitching to me about extra cars on your damn caboose. Sorry, Jane."

A FEW MINUTES LATER Marcus and Antoine came back in and plunked down in the comfortable chairs. Marcus crossed his legs, picked off a thread from his lavender pants, and let out a huge sigh.

"What's your problem?" Margo asked.

"Another near fashion fatality, Sister, darling. The little swipes at the factory covered one of the chairs in tweed when it was supposed to be brocade. How can you not know the difference between a tweed and a brocade?" he said, fanning himself. Then, looking at Antoine, he added, "Not that Edwina would ever know the difference."

Katie, who was still heavily engrossed in studying her butt, whipped around.

"What did you just say?"

"I said those little swipes at the factory don't know the difference…"

"No, after that. What did you say?"

"I said Edwina wouldn't know the difference. The woman wouldn't know the difference between a hand-painted toile and a hand towel."

"Marcus, by any chance would you be referring to Edwina Sumner?" Katie asked.

Marcus cocked his head back. "You know her, darling?" he asked curiously.

"Do you?" Katie asked back.

"Of course I do. It takes a bitch to know one."

Everyone sat around the conference room while Katie filled Marcus and Antoine in on the case. Normally, she would never discuss a case with anyone outside the agency, but the opportunity it presented was too good to pass up. Besides, she trusted Marcus and Antoine.

"So this young woman has lost her job, her house, and her baby," Katie explained.

"Unforgivable," Marcus said dramatically. Antoine nodded in agreement while he watched as Divinity crawled up Alexandria's leg.

"We've been trying to get closer to the Sumners, but weren't sure how. Now if you were willing to help us out..."

"Sweetie," Marcus started, "I think I speak for my beloved partner and all the other women of the world when I say we both fully understand what it's like to be sexually harassed. All I can say is thank God, gay is the new black. Yes, you may count us in."

Antoine nodded.

"But let me be clear," Marcus said, running his hand down his pants, "that I will not wear any of your little secret spy equipment if it breaks the flow of my ensemble."

"No problem there, Marcus," Katie said with a tad of sarcasm,. "I was thinking that you could just introduce us and we'd be undercover."

"As what, darling, the misfits?"

"No," Katie said, slightly annoyed, "magazine writers. That way we could get inside her house, do a little snooping around, and see if there's anything worth looking at more closely."

"Magazine writers? From an interior decorating magazine?" Marcus made no apology as he laughed heartily. Antoine joined him.

"What?" Katie asked.

"Katarina, darling, you trying to pretend you're an editor for an interior decorating magazine would be like me trying to pretend I'm with *Sports Illustrated.*" Looking at Antoine, he added, "Not that I don't like to play ball sometimes."

Antoine smiled.

"I'll have you know I worked undercover for years," Katie said, perturbed.

"And I'm sure you made a wonderful junkie or femme du noir, darling, but this is an entirely different venue," Marcus said. Then he put his hand on her cheek and said, "We're not dealing with white powder, darling, we're dealing with white powder rooms. I'm sorry, but you just don't have it."

"Have what?" she asked.

Marcus rolled his eyes. "The look. The It Factor. The *je ne sais quois*. The style. She'd out you faster than I was at summer camp."

"You could teach me," Katie said.

"She thinks I'm Dr. Doolittle," he said to Antoine as he reached for Katie's hand and stood her up.

"It isn't just knowing the lingo, darling, it's about the look and you—" he poked at her shoulders and breasts, "—you just don't have it. I'm so sorry, darling, but no. It simply won't work."

Katie sat down and announced, "I'm just warning all of you that if one more person makes a crack about my body…remember that I have a gun and I know how to use it."

"Tsk tsk," Marcus said with no apologies. "And here they call it 'men'struation…'"

Katie glared at Marcus. Margo tried to suppress a laugh.

"She could do it," Antoine said, nodding toward Alexandria. Marcus dropped Katie's hand, walked over, placed one finger on his cheek, and started circling around Alexandria like a shark on a feeding frenzy. Alexandria watched him nervously.

"How do you stay so thin, my little Spider Woman?" Marcus asked.

Katie threw up her hands in disgust. "Because she doesn't eat is how, unless you count diet soda or chocolate."

"I haven't seen her eat since 2002," Margo added. "Something to do with that damn cybermetabolism of hers. Must be some damn low frequency waves coming off the equipment or something."

Alexandria gave a small smile, but kept an eye on Marcus as he circled around.

"She does have the look, doesn't she?" Marcus said tapping his finger against his cheek.

Katie frowned. "Forget it," she said, "Alex doesn't do undercover work."

"I could teach her," Antoine offered. "Not the undercover part, but the interior decorator part."

"Absolutely not," Katie said.

"Why not?" Marcus asked.

"Because…It's just that…Alex doesn't…She's not…" Katie threw her hands up in the air. "She does computers. That's what Alex does. She does the computers and I do the undercover work."

"You let me deliver that stuff," Jane offered. "I was nervous, but it was a lot of fun once it was over."

"You made a delivery," Katie reminded her. "You weren't pretending to be something completely different." Katie saw the look on Jane's face and immediately offered an apology. "But you did do a great job, Janie," she added. It was a little too late.

"I've done undercover work before," added Margo.

"Yeah, you worked as a waitress in a restaurant for a week to get the goods on a cheating husband. That was a big stretch," Katie said sarcastically.

Marcus dropped back down in the chair. "Then I'm afraid we can't help you," he said.

They were all resigned to the discussion being over when Alexandria said very quietly, "I'll do it."

Katie whipped around at her. "Alex, you don't have to…"

"I said, I'll do it."

Katie bent down next to her. Divinity stirred from her resting spot on Alex's chest and began to move toward her. Katie gritted her teeth and stayed put.

"Alex," she began very gently. "You don't need to do this. You've never done the undercover part before and I'm not going to take any risks with anyone here getting hurt," she added.

"I'll do it," Alexandria said again. Then, turning to Antoine, she said, "You'll teach me?"

Antoine jumped up, "Class is in session," he said as he offered her his hand. Alexandria looked at his hand but didn't take it. Instead, she followed him obediently out the door to the offices of Sachet and Sashay.

Katie walked over to the bar, poured a good slug of scotch into a glass, and knocked it back in one swallow.

9

A FEW DAYS LATER, the white van, now with "Divinity Magazine" painted on the side, pulled up in the circular driveway of the Sumner house, followed by Marcus and Antoine in their black BMW.

"You're absolutely sure, Alex?" Katie asked from the back of the van. "You really don't have to do this," she emphasized.

Alexandria nodded but didn't say anything. Katie reached forward to check the pin-hole camera located in the spider brooch pinned to Alexandria's sweater. Alexandria recoiled at her touch.

"I'm sorry," Katie said, "but I need to check the camera one more time."

Alexandria averted her gaze as Katie tested the camera. Then she picked up her cell phone and spoke into it.

"Testing, testing," Katie said. Alexandria winced as the tiny receiver embedded in her ear rang out.

"Sorry about that," Katie said. "I forgot how sensitive it was."

Alexandria rubbed at her ear.

"You have it?" Katie asked.

Alexandria reached into her pocket and took out what appeared to be a pen. She opened the cap up to reveal a small device with a USB port on the end of it.

"How much time will you need?" Katie asked.

"It depends on how many files I need to download."

"And all you do is stick it in the USB port?"

"That's it."

"Okay," Katie said. "Just remember what I told you."

"Ten percent acting, ninety percent attitude," Alexandria repeated.

"That a girl," Katie said and she ducked into the back of the van to monitor everything going on. Alexandria placed the pen back in her pocket, picked up the clipboard with the hidden microphone in it, and stepped out.

"EDWINA, DARLING," MARCUS SAID as they exchanged kisses on both cheeks. "You remember Antoine, don't you?" Marcus said as Edwina also kissed Antoine on both cheeks. "And this is Alexandria Arachnius, one of the writers for *Divinity* magazine."

Katie froze. If Edwina tried to kiss Alexandria it was all over. Alexandria quickly offered her hand. "How do you do, Mrs. Sumner," she said.

"It's Edwina." The two women shook hands.

Katie let out a small sigh of relief.

Marcus jumped in. "As I explained to you on the phone, Edwina, darling, Alexandria is doing a special feature on mixing styles. She's just dying to get a look at some of our *fait accompli*. And don't hate her because she's so thin. Ex-model and all that," Marcus added.

Katie winced because that wasn't in the script.

"Really?" Edwina said curiously. "Who did you model for?"

Katie watched from the hidden buttonhole camera on Antoine's shirt as Alexandria swallowed hard.

"Didn't you say it was Donna Karan?" Antoine offered.

"Yes," Alexandria said.

"I love Donna Karan," Edwina said. "In fact, this suit is hers, but of course you already knew that."

Alexandria glanced at Edwina's blue suit with little interest and said, "Of course."

"I'm not familiar with your magazine," Edwina began. "What styles do you cover?"

Alexandria ignored her and strolled casually around the room as she answered. "You haven't seen it because it's new, but you'll be seeing our first issue on the stands soon. We're up against the usual, *Beautiful Homes, Interior Design, BH&G*. We cover many different styles from classical to haute couture."

"Good girl," Katie said out loud to no one.

"I see," Edwina said, "and is there any particular style that you're looking for now? Marcus and Antoine have given me quite an eclectic mix."

They all waited. Finally, Alexandria turned and said, "I'd like to see a convergence of old and new. Neo-classic with a touch of modernism."

"Then she must see Donald's office," Marcus emphasized.

Edwina hesitated. "Donald doesn't like people in his office. Confidential business matters and all that," she said waving her hand.

Katie gritted her teeth.

Alexandria ignored her and strolled over to the fireplace. She picked up a silver photo frame from the mantle.

"That's my son, Anthony," Edwina began. "He works with Donald at Sumner Design."

"And this?" she asked, holding the picture of a little girl.

"That's my granddaughter, Vanessa."

"She's lovely," Alexandria said.

"Precious," Marcus added as he glanced over Alexandria's shoulder.

"She's been through a great deal, poor child," Edwina said, but offered nothing more as she took a long drag on her cigarette and blew a spiral of smoke toward them. Alexandria stifled a small cough.

"I'd like to see the rest of the house now, if you don't mind," she said as she carefully placed the photo back in its place.

Katie watched through the monitors as Edwina brought them from room to room.

"Wait until you see the mix of French Country and French Classic in the living room," Marcus offered. "You'll have a gasm for sure," he said. Alexandria nodded.

They passed a closed room and Alexandria put her hand on the door and said, "May I?"

"Oooh," Edwina said, hesitating, "Donald really doesn't like anyone in his office."

"Edwina, darling," Marcus began, "we worked so hard on that room and that's probably just what the magazine is looking for."

Edwina took a long drag from her cigarette. "Just a quick look, then," she said. She opened the door. Alexandria's eyes went immediately to the laptop computer on the solid mahogany desk.

"It's fabulous," Alexandria said. "The vaulted ceilings combined with the asymmetrical alignment of the furniture juxtapose each other so well," she said. Antoine gave a small smile.

"Do you think so?" Edwina said.

"It's simply faboo," Alexandria said.

Katie laughed out loud inside the van.

"See then? She must write up this room."

"Well, I suppose…"

"Good. It's all settled. Now Edwina, darling, I desperately need you to show me what ideas you had for the dining room and if I don't have a lovely little drink in my hands soon, I'm bound to wilt," Marcus said as he put his hand under her elbow and led her toward the door.

"I'm not sure that she should…" Edwina began.

Alexandria ignored them all as she glanced from wall to wall, writing furiously on her notepad.

"It's just that Donald…" Edwina tried again.

"I smell a cover story here," Alexandria said.

Edwina stopped. "Really?" she asked.

"Not just any cover," Alexandria continued, "The inaugural cover."

"Way to go, Alex," Katie, suitably impressed, muttered to herself.

"Oh my," Edwina said as she took the cigarette from her mouth and put her hand to her chest. "The inaugural cover," she repeated.

"Now come along, Edwina Darling, and let our clever friend write her story while we three have a tete-a-tete about the dining room."

Marcus and Antoine led Edwina out. Alexandria waited all of ten seconds before rushing over to the desk and flipping the power to the laptop on. It had a boot password on it, but she had come prepared for that. She slipped an emergency startup disk from her pocket into the drive and bypassed the bootup password. Alex then opened the pen-like device and stuck it into the USB port in the back of the laptop. Immediately, files began to transfer. She looked around the room nervously. She could hear the voices retreating.

"You're safe," Katie whispered into the cell phone. "They're down at the other end of the house." Alexandria gave a small nod.

Katie switched to the monitor that showed the view from the tiny camera on Antoine's jacket. Marcus had indeed refused to wear anything. Antoine wasn't thrilled about wearing anything either, but when Katie explained to him that it would provide backup safety to Alexandria, he agreed.

"You know what would look simply divine right here?" Marcus asked. "An Aubusson."

"What's that?" Edwina asked.

"Handmade French tapestries that are used for wall hangings as well as carpets. I see a beautiful French landscape right here," he said sweeping his arm.

Edwina glanced nervously around the room. "Do you think she's done yet?"

"Genius can't be rushed," Marcus said. "Now what was in your clever mind for window treatments?"

"I don't know," she said stabbing the air with her cigarette. "A jabot, perhaps?"

"Hmmm…" Marcus said as he tapped his finger on his chin. "What do you think, Antoine, my Adonis?"

Antoine glanced nervously at the door for a second before responding, "Yes, a jabot," he said.

"Aren't you the clever one?" Marcus said. Just as the words were uttered, Katie heard the sound of a car. She watched as a late-model Jaguar slowed down by the van and pulled in behind Marcus and Antoine's BMW. There was no mistaking the silvery hair as Donald Sumner stepped out and glanced curiously at the white van. Much to Katie's dismay, he began walking toward it. With nowhere else to hide, she hit the floor and curled herself up behind the passenger seat. Donald Sumner looked in the van, saw no one there and strolled off toward the house.

Katie waited until she was certain he was out of earshot. "Heads up," Katie whispered into the cell phone. "Donald Sumner just pulled up. Do you copy, Alex?"

"Copy," Alexandria whispered back.

"Pull it out if you have to," Katie said. "Just stick with your story," she responded as calmly as she could.

"Can't. It's not done," Alex whispered back a little louder.

"That's okay," Katie said. "We'll get it another time," but she knew they wouldn't get another chance like this.

"Can't," she heard back.

"Antoine, Darling?" Antoine heard Marcus say again. "Earth to my Space Cadet," Marcus teased. Turning to Edwina Sumner, Marcus said, "He gets so caught up in the space."

"Tapestry or linen?" Marcus asked again.

"Oh," Antoine said as he was still trying to process what he'd just heard in the tiny microphone in his ear. "Tapestry, I guess," he answered with no idea what the question was. Marcus looked curiously at him wondering what was wrong.

Edwina glanced at the door as she heard her name called. "Donald!" she said, rather surprised. Donald Sumner strolled into the dining room and fanned the air with his hand. "Honestly, Edwina, I thought we had a deal," he said as he took the cigarette from her hand, put it out on a crystal candy dish, and coldly kissed her cheek.

"They're still in the dining room," Katie reported to Alexandria.

"I'm still downloading," Alexandria said.

"I'll let you know if they move," Katie assured her. "But it's really okay if you have to pull it. We'll just go with what we've got."

"I know, dear," Edwina said smugly to her husband. "It was just this one time," she lied. "Donald, this is Marcus and Antoine, my interior decorators. This is my husband, Donald Sumner."

Donald Sumner gave a deliberately crushing grip of a handshake to both men. In retaliation, Marcus reached toward Donald Sumner's lapel and stroked at it.

"That's lovely. Italian linen?" Marcus said, getting very close to his face. Donald Sumner recoiled and stepped back. Marcus flashed his eyes at him.

"And what brings you home at such an early hour, dear?" Edwina asked.

"I'm not home, just picking something up that I thought I had taken with me," he said. "It was nice meeting all of you," Donald Sumner said as he turned on his heels. Before he left the room, he said, "Don't let her spend all of my money frivolously now."

"Where are you going?" Edwina called to him.

"To my office," he said over his shoulder.

"Wait!" Edwina said as she followed him out. Marcus and Antoine followed her.

"Okay, they're headed your way," Katie said. "Pull the thing and act normal," she added. She waited for a response but got none. "Alex, do you copy me? Pull the damn thing out."

"Not yet."

"Listen to me very carefully, Alex," Katie said, deliberately quieting her tone. "Yank the damn thing out and slip it in your pocket and move away, okay? Alex? Alex?"

Katie glanced at the monitors as she watched Donald Sumner stride down the long corridor to his office with Edwina behind him followed by Marcus and Antoine.

"Alex, he's thirty feet away," Katie said quietly. "Power the laptop down and walk away from it. Now!"

"Donald!" Edwina called. Katie was surprised by the frantic tone in her voice. Donald Sumner paused with his hand on his office door and turned around.

"What is it, Edwina?" he asked, none too sweetly.

"It just that, well…Marcus and Antoine brought an editor from an interior decorating magazine over and she's going to feature our house as the cover story for the first issue!" Edwina blurted out. Donald Sumner looked at her like he cared less. Marcus slid between Donald Sumner and the door.

"Isn't it exciting?" he asked clapping his hands. "Imagine this," he said sweeping widely, "the drama, the excitement. Oooh, I can't stand it."

Donald Sumner cleared his throat. "Sure, that's wonderful. Now if you'll excuse me, I really do need to grab what I left behind and get back to work," he said as he started to open the office door.

"Donald?" Edwina said, delaying him further. "The editor is in there."

Donald Sumner turned to her. "Edwina, how many times have I told you that no one is to go into my office," he said as he shoved Marcus aside and whipped open the door.

Katie, who had been shot once, threatened repeatedly, and assaulted more times than she could remember, felt her heart pounding in her chest as Donald Sumner threw open the door and marched into his office. Edwina, Marcus, and Antoine all followed him in.

Alexandria stood in the corner far away from the desk, her arms folded, staring up at the windows. "I do believe we have cover material here," she said very casually as she turned and looked at them all. Marcus and Antoine let out small sighs of relief.

"Excuse me," Donald Sumner said, walking up to her. "I'm Donald Sumner," he said at the sight of the tall, attractive woman. His demeanor transformed instantly as he looked her up and down.

"Alexandria Arachnius."

"What an interesting name," he said as he extended his hand. Alexandria hesitantly offered hers and was shocked when Donald Sumner leaned forward to kiss the back of it. "But a lovely one," he added.

Back in the van, Katie held her breath as she saw the pained expression cross Alexandria's face as Donald attempted to kiss her hand. Alexandria instinctively withdrew it and turned back to the windows.

"Forgive me," he said apologetically.

Neither Marcus nor Antoine could get over his brazen flirting in the presence of his wife.

"Didn't you say you were in a hurry, Donald?" Edwina pouted.

Donald Sumner cleared his throat. "Yes, yes I did," he said as he walked over to his desk. "I could have sworn I put this in my bag this morning," he said as he picked up his laptop and carefully placed it inside his briefcase. "A pleasure to meet you," he said again, smiling at Alexandria. "I'm sure Edwina will want to celebrate our good fortune with a party or something. Perhaps you can join us."

"Perhaps," Alexandria said noncommittally. "I have several assignments and will be traveling quite a bit over the next few months. But one never knows…"

"You will send me advance copies of the article?" Edwina asked.

"Of course."

"I can't wait to read it."

"Oh, it will be quite a story," Alexandria said. "That I promise you."

Katie waited patiently for Alexandria to emerge and hop into the driver's seat. As they headed away, she asked, "Were you able to get anything?"

Alexandria glanced at her from the rearview mirror and gave a small smile as she reached into her pocket and held up the memory stick.

"It's full."

"That'a girl," Katie said.

"The secret," Margo began, "is to never let the cream or the milk get too hot and boil over," she said as she stirred the whisk briskly. They all sniffed the air and hunched over the pot as the last traces of bittersweet chocolate melted into it. "Did you know," she said, "that when Christopher Columbus brought back cocoa beans from the New World, King Ferdinand, said 'never mind, just show us the gold?'"

"Asshole," Katie said. Then, giving Jane an apologetic look, she corrected herself and said, "Sorry—idiot."

"How would he have known there was value in a bean?" Jane asked.

"I don't care who brought it over," Margo said as she stirred, "I'm just damn glad they did."

"And I'm just glad it has no calories," Katie said and they all laughed. They had a pact that anything made with chocolate "had no calories."

They all took their places around the island as Margo carried the pot over. First she added a dash of cinnamon and then, using a grater, added a tiny bit of nutmeg. She reached underneath and pulled out a bottle of Kahlúa, which she slowly stirred in. They licked their lips as she carefully poured the hot chocolate into four cups. She topped each cup with a dollop of fresh whipped cream, then dusted that with a little cocoa powder.

Each woman, in turn, raised her cups.

"To Alexandria Axelrod, Ace Detective," Katie said. "Or should I say, 'Alexandria Arachnius,' for her first successful undercover mission."

"Here, here," Jane said.

"Way to go, Alexandria," Margo said. "You'll be giving Katie a run for her money now."

Alexandria gave a small smile. "It was kind of fun, now that it's over," she said quietly.

"I felt the same way," Jane said. "I was such a nervous wreck when I had to deliver those packages, but when it was over, I felt such a…rush."

"You sure you weren't just having one of your damn hot flashes?" Margo teased.

They all took a long, slow sip of the rich, chocolatey broth, then burst out laughing as they looked at each other. Each woman had a big, foamy, whipped-cream mustache on her upper lip.

10

Katie locked the door to the bathroom, shrugged off her blazer ,and stepped into the shower fully dressed. The two mirrors surrounded by the Moroccan tile gave a fairly accurate three-dimensional view. She turned this way and that and let out a long sigh. Her once-taut body was definitely becoming soft and truth be told, her slacks had become snugger lately. When she was in her twenties, she didn't have to do much to stay in shape. Now at age thirty-eight, that had all changed. She shook her head and stepped back out.

Alexandria came into the conference room with Divinity poised on her shoulder. She sat down in the empty chair next to Jane. Jane immediately stiffened and edged her way toward the back of her seat.

"You got an e-mail," Alexandria said to Katie, who was reading through a file.

"From who?" Katie asked, looking up.

"Mrs. Barnett."

"The wife of Mr. Sweet Peaches?" Katie asked.

"Yes."

"Bring it up," she said. "I can't wait to see what she thought of the video."

Jane, who had been reading *The Wall Street Journal*, set it aside and looked up at the big monitor.

The e-mail popped up on-screen.

"Dear Katie," it began, "I cannot thank you all enough for the outstanding work your agency did. My attorney was quite pleased, indeed, to receive the copy of the video and the e-mails. Upon mentioning it and its content to Paul's attorney, they offered an immediate settlement, which, as you recommended, we rejected. A counter offer was made and, needless to say, I am quite pleased with it. Paul has since moved out, at my request, to greener pastures, or in his case, perhaps I should say, 'orchards.' My only regret is that I will no longer get the satisfaction of cleaning the toilet every day with his toothbrush. What a clever idea! With Warmest Regards, Elinor Barnett."

Katie smiled satisfactorily.

"Who suggested she clean the toilet with her husband's toothbrush?" Jane asked.

They all looked at Katie.

"You didn't," Jane said.

Katie laughed. "Oh, come on, Janie, it was kind of a joke, but maybe she took me seriously. In any case, he got what he deserved and now, so will she."

Jane looked at her aghast. "How unsanitary, Katie. He could have gotten sick."

Katie stopped smiling. "Come on, Janie, I said it was a joke. I didn't think she'd really do it. She's probably just kidding about it." Just then, Katie's cell phone began to vibrate. As she was reaching for it, Jane asked, "Katie, could I talk to you in private for a minute?"

Upon seeing the number on the screen, Katie was deaf to Jane's request.

"Hello?" Katie said. "Yes, this is she. Is everything all right?" They watched her face as an immediate look of concern came across it. "I see," she said. "No, I understand. I'll be there right away."

"Is everything all right?" Margo asked.

Katie grabbed for her blazer. "It had better be," she said as she walked out.

KATIE PULLED UP TO Shamrock Shores and noticed the silver Volvo parked two spots down. "Oh great," she thought to herself.

Her sister, Kelly Mahoney-Dwyer, was seated next to her mother in the director's office. Her mother looked up at her and gave a small smile reminiscent of a child in the principal's office.

"Hello, dear," Molly said as Katie bent down to kiss her mother on the cheek. Katie could smell the Jack Daniels easily on her mother's breath; her cheeks were flushed and her pupils were slightly dilated.

Katie glanced over at her sister, who sat with her hands folded across her very swollen belly. She saw the tight jaw, a sure sign that

Kelly was perturbed. Kelly glanced over at Katie for a second before turning back to the director, Gracelyn MacDougal. Katie took the chair on the opposite side of her mother.

"Now that you're all here," Gracelyn MacDougal began, "I want to say that we do enjoy having Molly here as one of our residents; in fact, she's well-liked by everyone, which makes this all the more difficult."

Katie glanced at her mother, who immediately lowered her head.

"But there seems to be some confusion about the rules here at Shamrock Shores. As you both knew when you brought your mother to us, Shamrock Shores is a 'dry' community. I believe that was made very clear, both in our orientation and in our brochures."

"It was made very clear," Kelly said as she leaned forward and glared at Katie.

"We're not police officers," Gracelyn MacDougal said, glancing at Katie, "but it is very apparent that your mother has been… imbibing, shall we say."

"Gracelyn," Molly Mahoney began to say, but Kelly immediately put her hand on her mother's arm.

"Let her finish, Mother," Kelly said, "and I'll remind you again that you are not obligated to say anything."

"Spoken like a true defense attorney," Katie muttered under her breath. Kelly heard her and shot her a cross look.

"We realize that for some this is a difficult rule to abide by, which is why we make it so very clear in all of our literature and discussions," Gracelyn MacDougal said. "Even so, we might look the other way for an occasional isolated incident; however…"

"She got the whole floor tanked," Kelly blurted out. "It seems someone," she stopped and stared at Katie for a second or two, "smuggled her a couple of bottles of Jack Daniels and they all decided to have a party."

"It's not that we're a bunch of evangelists," Gracelyn MacDougal explained. "I, myself, enjoy an occasional glass of wine, but many of the residents here are on very strong medications. We promote Shamrock Shores as a 'dry' facility so that the families of the residents know that their loved ones are receiving the best care possible. We simply cannot afford to take a chance that someone will have a medication interaction."

Just then, Katie's phone began to vibrate. She saw the BWA number appear on the screen but ignored it and tucked it back into her pocket.

"Did someone have a medication interaction?" Katie asked.

"Well, no…not this time, but of course they're all on different medications and those prescriptions change all the time."

"And is my mother on any medication?" Katie asked.

Gracelyn MacDougal was caught off-guard.

"Well, no, but the rules apply to everyone, regardless."

"Of course they do," Kelly said sympathetically.

Relieved to have someone on her side, Gracelyn MacDougal said gratefully, "Thank you for understanding."

Katie looked at her mother, who remained with her head down.

"Ma?" she asked gently. "Are you okay?"

Molly Mahoney looked up at her daughter and said, "Oh, yes, dear."

"So what happens now?" Kelly asked. Subconsciously, she rubbed her hand around in circles over her engorged belly.

"Well," Gracelyn MacDougal began, "because Molly is so well-liked around here, we're willing to make this one exception, but I must tell you that we are putting you—" she glanced at Katie, "all of you, on notice that if it happens again, we'll have no choice but to ask her to leave. I'm sorry, but it's for the benefit of everyone."

Kelly grabbed both arms of the chair and pushed herself up slowly. "I assure you it will not happen again, Mrs. MacDougal," she said as she finally got to her feet and shook the woman's hand.

They escorted their mother back to her small room.

KELLY WAITED UNTIL HER mother was in the bathroom before she said, "For God's sakes, Katie, what were you thinking?"

"What do you mean, 'what was I thinking?'"

"Are you denying you brought her the booze?" Kelly demanded.

"I'm not denying, nor am I admitting anything," Katie said.

Katie looked at her sister, saw the very flushed cheeks and the irritated look on her face.

"They have rules," Kelly began. "And you knew about it before we placed her here."

"This was your idea!" Katie said. "Ma didn't even want to come here. She wanted to live with you, but you're too busy to take her," Katie said, trying to control the volume of her voice.

"I can't, for God's sakes," Kelly said. "With the kids and Tom and work and the new baby, I just can't. She's safe here. We both agreed she'd do best here. What were you thinking!"

"You want to know what I was thinking?" Katie said, glancing at the bathroom door. "I was thinking that at her age, she has the right to do whatever the hell she wants to do. That's what I was thinking."

"It figures you would feel that way," Kelly said.

"Meaning what?" Katie asked, whipping back around.

"Meaning that when it comes to this whole situation, the fermented apple doesn't fall far from the tree." Katie turned her back. "Katie," her sister said in a much softer tone, "hey, I didn't mean it like that."

Katie stared out the window in an attempt to slow her breathing.

"Look, Katie, I'm just exhausted and I feel like shit. I'm sorry."

"Sorry for what?" their mother asked as she came back out of the bathroom.

"Nothing," Katie said, looking at her sister. Then to her mother, "Look, Mom, maybe this isn't the right place for you."

"But I like it here," Molly Malone said. "I like all of the people."

Katie remembered Mr. Timothy Collins. "I know you do, Ma," she said gently, "but it doesn't look like they're going to back down on their rules."

"Jesus, Mary, and Joseph," their mother said with her trace of a brogue, "I'm too old to live by rules."

"I agree, Ma," Katie said. She saw the look Kelly gave her. "But maybe we can try and work a little better within the rules. You know, stick with Annie Timmons' pot roast for now."

Kelly looked at them both curiously. Molly Mahoney placed her hand on her daughter's arm.

"All right, Katie," she said in a child-like voice.

Katie could see her mother was tired. "Do you want to lie down?" she asked. Molly Mahoney nodded.

The two sisters walked out of Shamrock Shores in silence. As they reached the parking lot, Kelly turned and said, "The girls have been asking for their Aunt Katie. Why don't you swing by the house later on and see them?"

Katie put her sunglasses on. "Thanks anyway, but I'm in the middle of something."

"Katie," Kelly began to say, but Katie turned her back and walked away.

11

Katie walked into the office and was surprised to find no one manning the front desk. She peered into the cybercision center, but Alex wasn't there. She glanced at Jane's office and found it empty. She swung open the heavy mahogany doors of the conference room. Margo stood up immediately and glanced worriedly at Alexandria.

"What's going on?" Katie asked.

"We have a problem," Alexandria said as she nodded toward Margo. Margo reached into her pocket and took out an envelope with Katie's name on the front of it.

"Dear Katie," the letter began. "I want to apologize for not being there in person to deliver this, but you were called away. It is with deep regret that I am submitting my resignation. Due to circumstances beyond my control, I do not feel I can continue my employment at the BWA. I want to thank you for all of your support during difficult personal circumstances. Regards, Jane Landers."

Katie reread the note several times and looked up at Margo and Alexandria. "That's it?" she asked. They both nodded. "She didn't say anything?"

"Just that she was sorry and she'd miss us," Alexandria said.

"We tried to stop her," Margo said. "We tried calling you."

Katie shook her head. "That's okay," she said as she remembered her phone going off during the meeting at Shamrock Shores. Katie turned to leave.

"Where are you going?" Margo asked.

"Where do you think?" Katie answered.

KATIE BROKE A FEW speed limits on her way over to Jane's house in the quiet neighborhood of South Granger. She pulled up in front of a small white cape replete with picket fence. Jane's car was in the driveway.

Katie waited for several minutes before Jane came to the door. She had pink floral gardening gloves on that were covered in dirt.

"Katie," Jane said, looking rather red-faced. "I'm sorry. I was out back in the garden. Won't you come in, please?"

Most of the windows were open, even on this cool day. Katie wrapped her jacket around her a little tighter.

Noticing this, Jane offered, "Would you like a cup of hot tea? I'm afraid I have to keep it rather cool in here these days. Or perhaps you'd like something stronger?"

"Tea's fine, Jane."

A few minutes later, Jane set a tray with a pot of tea down on a small side table. Angel, Jane's large white cat, popped out of nowhere and curled up in Jane's lap. The cat purred contentedly as Jane stroked its ears.

"I suppose you came here because you read my letter," Jane began.

"I did."

"I'm sorry I didn't wait for you to be there, Katie. If you require it, I'll come back to complete two weeks…"

"What I'd prefer, Janie, is that you come back for good."

"But I can't, Katie. I'm sorry, but I just can't."

Jane brushed the perspiration from her forehead back toward her gray hair.

"I'm sorry, Katie, can you excuse me for a minute?" she asked.

Jane came back with a white linen embroidered cloth and a glass of ice water.

"Are you all right?" Katie asked.

Jane shook her head. "This is miserable, Katie. I don't mean to complain, but when the hot flash kicks in, I feel like I'm burning up from the inside out." Katie watched as Jane picked up the glass of ice water and instead of putting it to her lips, put it to her neck.

"That must feel awful," Katie said sympathetically.

"It is. It's very confusing, too. I don't know what's going on with my body half the time. Sometimes I feel like my heart is pounding and I feel very anxious. It's a difficult time, but I'll get through it."

"Can't your doctor give you anything for it?"

"She has," Jane said, "but you can't completely medicate away what Mother Nature intends."

Katie sipped her tea. "So, Jane, tell me why you really left."

"It's complicated, Katie, but what it comes down to is this: I'm just not comfortable working there anymore."

"Look, Janie, if it's that damned spider, I'll make Alex keep it at home…"

"It's not the spider, although I must say it does give me quite a stir at times."

"Then what is it?"

"It's you."

Katie lowered her cup.

"Me?"

"Yes."

"I don't understand."

"Do you remember when we first met, Katie?"

"Sure."

"George had just taken off and I came to file a missing persons report. You worked tirelessly for three weeks to locate him. You comforted me when I thought he was dead. You gently broke the news to me that he had left me penniless and gone to Bermuda with that—that woman. I was deeply indebted to you—I still am Katie, for all of your professionalism and concern," Jane sipped her ice water and held the glass to her throat. "And then you gave me a job when no one else would hire me because of my age. I want you to know that I do appreciate all of that. But things have changed. It's all changed."

"What's changed?"

"You. The way you operate. The lengths you'll go to find out information. The laws you'll break to get that information. You used to uphold the law, Katie, and I respected you for that."

"And don't think I don't know about where the money comes from," Jane said. Katie looked away. "You think I don't know, but I'm the one who manages the books, Katie. It's an endless supply."

"I don't know where she gets the money," Katie said. "I honestly don't."

"But you must know that it can't possibly come from legitimate sources."

"Look, Janie," Katie said, "I'm going to be real honest here with you. There's a lot about Alex that I don't know, don't get. But she was in the same boat as the rest of us and she's dedicated and loyal to getting the job done. For all I know she could be the daughter of a billionaire. I don't press her for details about her personal life because she's not comfortable providing them."

"I understand that," Jane said, "but if we're ever audited…"

"If we're ever audited," Katie began, "it's my signature on all of the accounts payable and receivable. I'll take my chances if it means getting things done." She cradled the teacup in her hands. "Look, Janie, if things have changed on how we conduct business, it's only because sometimes the rules have to change. You're right, I upheld the law for twelve years. I was sworn to uphold it and I did. The women who come to us as clients know that if they want the case to be run within the boundaries of the law, we'll do that. Look at all the cases we've testified at in court. Look at all the times I've secured releases from clients and obtained warrants before searches and testified to chain of custody on computer forensic evidence. I'm not opposed to staying within the rules and limits of the law if that's what the client wants and that's what the case warrants. But sometimes things just don't work out that way."

Angel arched her back and turned to face Katie.

"You know what, Janie? Despite being a very good cop, I took a hit to my stomach and my career and no one ever paid for that, but even though I got, excuse me, screwed over by my own people, I'm still willing to work within the law whenever we can. I'm not trying to circumvent anything, Janie, but you've seen the women who come to us. Many have supported their husbands for years and stand to lose everything. They're desperate, Janie."

"Desperate for what, Katie?" Janie asked. "Getting justice or getting revenge?"

A LITTLE WHILE LATER, Katie sent a text message to Alexandria and Margo.

It read, "Not coming back to the office today—KM."

Margo read it and looked at Alexandria. "You'll keep an eye on her?" she asked.

Alexandria nodded.

Working quickly, Margo sautéed the brown bread cubes in melted butter. Setting them aside, she sautéed fresh sliced mushrooms and began to layer them in the casserole dish along with the deveined shrimp and shredded cheese. She carefully poured a layer of cream over the entire mixture and sprinkled fresh black pepper, a little salt, and a dash of paprika on top. Satisfied, she covered the dish and tucked it in the oven. She reached for the bottle of Chardonnay and began to open it.

Calvin came up from behind her and slid his hands around her waist.

"Something smells mighty fine," he said as he nuzzled at her neck.

Margo turned around and looked into his warm brown eyes. "It will take over an hour to bake," she said. "You think you can wait that long?"

"I don't know," he said, touching her cheek. "I'm very, very hungry."

She laid her hands on his arms.

"What you hungry for, sugar?" she asked, her eyes flashing.

"This," he said, as he leaned forward and kissed her.

Margo closed her eyes.

"When will Trevor be home?" he asked quietly.

She glanced at the clock. "He's at his friend's house for another three hours."

"And the food will take how long?" he asked as he slid his mouth down her neck.

She pulled him closer. "We have an hour before it's cooked," she said teasingly.

"Then I suggest we do our own cooking," he said as he gently edged her out of the kitchen toward her bedroom. His kisses grew firmer along with a few other things as he brought her down to the bed and rolled on top. She began to unbutton his shirt when he suddenly pulled away.

"What was that?" he asked.

Margo sighed. "Hang on a minute," she said as she pushed him away and dug deep into her pocket for the tiny receiver that was vibrating. She flipped open a small screen and read the four words, "Third hour, Blue Line," that appeared on the text message. She winced.

"Is everything okay?" Calvin asked gently.

She sat up. "Damn. I am so sorry, Cal, but I gotta take care of a friend. Can you stay here and wait for Trevor to get home? If I'm not home by then, can you call Marcus and ask him to come over and get him? The casserole can come out in an hour…"

"But Baby, I thought we could…"

"I know," she said, kissing him affectionately on the cheek. "Believe me, I wouldn't pass this up if it wasn't important. Will you be okay?"

He slipped his arms back around her waist. "I will if you come back here as soon as possible."

Alexandria's messages were always short but the fact that Alexandria had even sent it meant she was worried.

"Damn her," Margo thought to herself. Calvin was the first decent man she'd met in a long time. He had a steady job as a manager of a construction company. He liked Trevor a lot, which meant the world to Margo, and was a regular attendee at her church, which is where they first met. More importantly, Katie insisted that they run him from one end to the other and he came out squeaky clean.

Margo paused at the front entrance of the Blue Line Bar to let her eyes adjust to the dark, smoky room. She glanced over at Sean, the owner, who was polishing a glass with what looked like a dirty cloth. Sean spotted her and tipped his head toward the private backroom, called "The House," where only cops were allowed. Margo stepped around the tables and went through the door. The music was loud. She recoiled at the smell. It was like being trapped inside a whiskey barrel.

Margo saw Katie standing on top of a table, clutching a glass, dancing for her audience. The top three buttons of her sweater were undone, revealing the edges of her black bra and ample bosom. The men sat around the table with drinks in their hands cheering her on.

"Come on, Katie," one of them shouted, "show us what you got."

"How 'bout a strip search, Katie?" another one yelled.

Margo shook her head, shoved her way through them, and grabbed Katie by the hand.

"Hey," Katie yelled as her drink spilled down her sweater. Margo yanked her hard and she practically fell off the tabletop. One of them, a tall guy who was a little less drunk than the rest, caught her in his arms as she came down.

"How 'bout I give you a ride home, Katie?" he asked as his hands slipped from her waist to her sweater. The men cheered him on.

"I dunno, got your cuffs on you?" Katie slurred back as she smiled and touched him on the chest. Then, spotting Margo for the first time, she said, "Hey, here's my friend. Any of you boys like dark meat?"

"Come on, Katie," Margo said, "let's get the hell out of here," but the tall one would not let go.

"Take your damn hand off of her," Margo ordered as she grabbed Katie by the arm.

"I will when I feel like it," he said with whiskey breath.

"She needs to go home," Margo said as she pulled. The man pulled right back. They started their own game of tug of war as Margo tried to pull Katie out and he pulled her back.

"Hey, we're dancing," Katie said as she swayed back and forth.

Before Margo knew what was happening, several of the men grabbed her from behind. One hand slid down her leg. She turned to see who the offender was and lost hold of Katie's arm as she felt several arms grab hold of her. When she realized Katie could not, was not, going to defend herself, she began to panic. Margo turned and tried to pull away, but several of them held her. She felt another hand go up her skirt.

"Y'all better leave me the fuck alone!" she yelled, trying to get their attention, but they were all too drunk to listen. She looked over as the man who had Katie, pulled her back against him, leaned into her and kissed her on the neck.

She tried to wrench free.

"This one's a fighter," one of them said. "I like that."

"Come on, honey," another said. "We won't hurt you. We just want to have a little fun."

"Any friend of Katie's is a friend of ours," another said.

"If she's your friend, then get your damn hands off her and let her go," Margo shouted.

"Hey, Katie!" one of them yelled "Are we your friends?"

"You're my bess friends," Katie slurred.

"See? She wants to be here. Nobody's hurting her," they said. Once again, Margo tried to wrestle away from them. Hands grew tighter around her arms and then a hand was around her waist and she suddenly found herself being hoisted up on the table.

"Come on, honey, how about you do a quick dance for us and we'll let you go."

Just then, a very loud, deep voice from the doorway shouted, "Let them go right now!"

Margo looked toward the doorway. She immediately hopped off the table and straightened out her clothes. The men backed off.

"Sorry, Cap," several of the men said as they sat back down.

"You assholes will be lucky if you're not all facing an internal investigation by the morning. Now I suggest you get the hell out of here and go home to your families. The party's over."

IT WASN'T THE FIRST time they had met and each time, Margo was taken aback by just how good-looking Joe Kennedy was, for a white man, that is. He had wavy brown hair, a thick dark mustache, and green eyes. She could well understand how Katie must have fallen hard for him. He stepped forward and forcefully grabbed Katie by the elbow. He tried to grab Margo, too, but she quickly yanked her arm away and followed him out the door.

AS THEY PASSED THE bar, Margo stopped to settle the tab. Sean waved her off and said, "She's all set," to which Margo replied, "That's part of the problem." He just shrugged.

IT HAD BEEN FOURTEEN years since Katie and Sean McCleary were partners. Katie was still a rookie and Sean, a seasoned cop on the verge of retirement, protested to anyone who would listen about being stuck with "a little girl" for a partner. That is, until one fateful night when that "little girl" saved his ass. What should have been an ordinary motor vehicle stop ended up in a shootout with a suspect who had enough warrants to not want to go back to prison. Katie, new and green but with academy training still fresh in her blood, watched nervously as her partner, the seasoned cop, turned his back on the driver to lean down and inspect a broken headlight. Katie, who was standing guard at the corner of the car as she had been trained to do, saw the driver reach his right hand beneath the seat. With all of her senses heightened, she watched almost in slow motion as she saw the glint and shape of a semi-automatic pistol emerge. As it had been drilled over and over to her at the academy, she screamed "gun!" as loud as she could, although the volume of her voice seemed choked. She drew her own weapon from her holster.

Sean glanced up at her choked call and watched with his mouth open as the first bullet fractured the windshield and flew past him by an inch. Within a second, the driver fired again. Sean frantically tried to take cover where there was none. He didn't even have time to draw his weapon before another shot rang out. Katie didn't shout, "Police, drop your weapon," because there was no time and no need. She just raised her duty weapon and squeezed the trigger. Forget about going for the head. The bigger target was his shoulders and that's exactly where the bullet landed, in his right shoulder blade. The driver slumped over and the weapon fell from his hand. Katie stood there motionless as the reality of what had happened sunk in. Sean reached for his shoulder mike and screamed, "Shots fired. We need an ambulance!" to dispatch. Katie remained motionless until the uncontrollable shaking began.

"Holy shit!" Sean said over and over. With gun drawn, he carefully opened the driver's door and removed the weapon from the suspect. He used a handkerchief on the barrel so as not to disturb any prints. Wounded or not, he pulled the suspect's hands together and cuffed him. He realized his error and looked up to see his little girl partner shaking from head to toe.

"It's okay, little girl. Sit down. It's okay. It's over. Holy shit," he said repeatedly for the fifty-eight seconds it took for a backup unit to roll up Code Three. Two ambulances arrived and after Katie and Sean were checked out, the EMTs declared the driver's wounds were not life-threatening, for which Katie was forever grateful. It was one thing to have to shoot someone, another to take a life and have to live with that. Katie refused to go to the hospital. Sean, who was a born storyteller, recounted the entire story to the street supervisor, a young sergeant named Joe Kennedy. Joe Kennedy realized, from the moment he rolled up on the scene, exactly what had happened, and knew that Sean McCleary was damned lucky to be alive and even luckier to have a sharp young partner who had just saved his ass. Thirteen hours later when internal affairs cleared Officer Kathleen Mahoney from any wrongdoing, she and Sean changed into their civilian clothes and headed to the nearest bar. It was the first time she got drunk and it felt damned good. Sean had already filed his retirement papers with the state retirement board. Much to Joe Kennedy's relief, Sean realized he didn't have it in himself anymore to be safe on the street. The very next day he bought the Blue Line Bar and swore that Katie Mahoney would never have to pay for a drink under his roof for as long as he lived.

As a brotherly gesture, Joe wrote the report so it wasn't too obvious that Sean had screwed up and included a recommendation to the chief that both officers be given a commendation for "duty above and beyond the call." The chief, realizing the political correctness and opportunity of it all, went beyond that and promoted the young female officer to the rank of detective, the youngest and most inexperienced officer ever to be promoted to detective in the history of the department. Katie was immediately transferred to the vice/narcotics division because they all knew with the girl-next-door Irish looks and the big boobs, few would suspect she was a cop. Katie reluctantly gave a two-page interview to a young reporter, Chelsea Mattox, who promised not to print any photos of Katie, nor describe her in any way that would give away her identity. She was referred to as "the young policewoman" over and over, a term that made Katie cringe.

Joe Kennedy made it his personal project to keep an eye on Katie and her big boobs and, since he was no longer her direct supervisor, offered to give her a few personal pointers. He became her "Rabbi," her trusted mentor whom she could turn to. His sessions as her department Rabbi grew more frequent and soon it was common knowledge that they were a "thing."

The sex was incredible. On the rare times when they both had a stretch of a few days off together, they'd spend almost the entire time in bed discovering each other. Many times their lovemaking was rushed with a passionate frenzy, but other times they lingered slowly in each other's arms. Occasionally they would shower and go out to eat, since Katie didn't cook, but they'd sit side by side in the restaurant and inevitably their hands would touch or Joe would casually brush up against her breasts and a whole new wave of lust would erupt and it was all they could do to get the server to bring the check before they were back in each other's arms once again. It was like that for the first few years, until Katie began to work more intense undercover assignments and Joe's responsibilities as a ranking supervisor grew. It wasn't so much that they grew apart, just that the more Katie worked undercover, the longer it took for her to shed her street-wise junkie persona when she came home.

She realized early on that having a few drinks usually brought her back to reality. In fact, the first few times she got drunk, the sex was even more amazing. She didn't have many inhibitions to begin with, but whatever was left completely disappeared. Joe never complained about anything as long as the sex was good. Over the course of their marriage, Joe began to talk about having children and settling down to a house in the country. Katie held him at bay, knowing full well that her career was at stake. Her reputation as an undercover cop grew, and she began to plunge deeper and deeper into the dark and dangerous world of illegal narcotics.

Joe worried for her. His supervisory position kept him safely parked behind a desk a good part of the shift while his wife strutted around on the back streets of the city co-mingling with desperate lives whose addictions made them dangerous and unpredictable. He would like to say he had complete faith in the narcotics division and the men who were assigned to keep his wife safe, but he had lost some faith in his wife's ability to keep herself safe all the time. Joe pressured her to ask for a transfer and they fought long and hard about it. Katie's only solace came from the bottle, and the more she drank to try and take the edge off everything, the more distant they became to each other. Joe's Irish temper got the better of him and hurtful words were exchanged. Joe was on days, and Katie worked the late afternoon well into the night when most of the deals were made in backrooms of seedy bars and down alleys. They soon became like two strangers living under the same roof. Whenever they were together, Katie chose her beloved Glenlivet over Joe.

Women were always coming on to cops. It was fairly common and though many took advantage of it, Joe did not. He was not a vain man, but understood he had a certain appeal to women that he for the most part ignored, making him that much more desirable. Rather than sitting home alone at night while Katie worked assignment after assignment, Joe would wander down to the local bar to grab a bite to eat and a couple of beers. Almost always, a woman would engage him in conversation when all he was trying to do was catch the game on the big screen. Normally, he'd politely ignore them and they'd get the hint, but lately he'd realized that was getting harder and harder to do, especially with the attractive ones.

One afternoon following a lengthy fight with Katie on the phone that ended with Katie screaming at him to "Go to hell," Joe had just hung up the phone when in walked Chelsea Mattox, who had been assigned to cover the police beat for the local paper. Her big smile and short skirt caught his attention immediately. For once, he was glad to see the press.

THEY REACHED MARGO'S CAR and, for the first time, Katie noticed him. Still swaying, she smiled, grabbed onto his shirt collar, and said, "Well, well, if it isn't my knight in shining armor. You wanna go party somewhere, Joe?"

Joe Kennedy opened the door and practically shoved Katie in. Margo watched him, but said nothing.

"Maybe I should follow you back to her place," he offered.

Margo whipped around to him. "That isn't necessary," she said tersely as she walked around to the driver's side.

Joe followed her around and stopped her from getting in. He put his arm across the doorframe. He first leaned in to check on

Katie, who sat slumped against the passenger side door. He turned around to face Margo.

"If you don't mind," Margo said as she tried to push his hand off her car door.

"For the thousandth time, I didn't set her up," he said desperately.

"Yeah, right, and you weren't cheating on her either, right? You were just a damn fine model of a husband."

Joe grabbed her under the elbow. "Look, not that this is any of your business or your concern, but I'm going to say this one more time. I may have broken some vows, but I never broke the law and I sure as hell did not set Katie up. It wasn't me."

For a second, she almost believed him.

"Yeah, right," Margo said, gathering herself together. "And I'm going to be the next president of the United States."

She practically shut the door on his hand as she jumped into her car. She glanced over at Katie, who was still slumped against the passenger door. Joe came around and before she could drive off, opened the passenger door, caught Katie as she nearly fell out, and buckled her safely into place.

"Take care of her," he said. Margo ignored him.

He backed off and stood watching as she peeled away.

MARGO DROVE KATIE BACK to the agency and led her into the "bain de femme," as Marcus called it. Sober, Katie could fight her way out of anywhere. Drunk, she was malleable.

"Come on, Katie," Margo said as she stripped Katie down to her underwear.

"Hey, you're not my type," Katie said as Margo steadied her.

"Trust me, that's one thing that doesn't run in the family," Margo answered. Katie grinned stupidly at her, not realizing what Margo was about to do. "Okay, here we go," Margo said as she shoved her in the shower.

"Oh no," Katie started to say when she realized what was happening, but Margo turned the faucet to the coldest setting and held the glass door tight.

Katie let out a series of curses that even Margo had never heard before as she banged furiously on the door to get out. Finally, Margo heard the words "Okay, okay, you win," and knew she'd had enough.

Katie stepped out, teeth chattering. She said very little as Margo wrapped her in a thick, terry-cloth robe and gave her a warm blanket to wrap around her. She led Katie to the conference room and sat her down in a chair while she went to make a fresh pot of hot, strong coffee.

Margo handed Katie the steaming cup and sat down opposite her. Katie's wet hair was a mess of curls. Margo thought she looked like a drowned poodle.

Katie took a deep breath. "How did you know where I was?" she said, wiping at her nose.

"Alexandria."

As her head began to clear, Katie remembered that their cell phones had Global Positioning Systems built into them to always detect their whereabouts. She also knew every inch of this room was covered by covert cameras and that Alex could very well be watching.

"Thanks a lot, Alex," Katie said as she gave the camera hidden in the recesses of the paneling the finger.

"Knock it off, Katie, she was worried about you," Margo said.

Katie nodded. "Okay, okay, I'm sorry, Alex," she said contritely as she waved toward the camera.

"And I'm worried about you," Margo said.

Katie looked away.

"Is this because of Jane?" Margo asked.

"No."

"Did you talk to her?" Margo asked.

"Yeah."

"And?"

"And I think I need to go home," Katie said as she started to get up, but Margo stopped her.

"You ain't going nowhere, girlfriend. Not till we talk about this."

Katie sat back down like a scorned child and threw her head back against the chair.

"She doesn't like the way we're doing business. She's uncomfortable with what we sometimes have to do to get the job done. She thinks I'm in it for revenge."

"Are you?"

"Am I what?" she asked, pretending she didn't understand the question.

"Are you in it for revenge?"

"If I was in it for revenge," she started, "then your ex would be behind bars or worse, Alexandria's hacker squeeze would be behind bars or worse, Jane's ex would be behind bars or worse, Joe…" Her voice trailed off.

"Okay, but she obviously has issues with it and we need to find a way to work around that."

"You tell me where the line between justice and revenge ends," Katie said.

Margo thought about that for a moment. "So she's not coming back?" she asked.

Katie sniffed. "I threw her resignation letter back at her and told her I wanted her to take some time off and reconsider. This damn menopause thing is making her act crazy. You'd think the doctors could give her a pill or something to make it better."

"She's damn scared, Katie. She doesn't understand what's going on and a lot of times she can't control any of it."

"You'd think with all this technology, they would be able to control it. Seems to me it's getting worse and worse."

"I'll remind you of that in twenty years."

"She's just…so easily offended sometimes. I don't know what her problem is."

"Really?" Margo asked. "We're just as damned offensive as some of the guys sometimes. We joke about the videos, we make fun of people…"

"But we don't force her to participate in any of it. That's the difference. You and I know we aren't going to be offended by it so it's okay." Katie shook her head. "Look, I'm fine now. I think I'll just head home. Sorry if I was any trouble."

"Katie," Margo started to say.

"I just overdid it a little, that's all. I'll go easy from now on. I swear."

"Katie," Margo said again.

"I may be in a little late in the morning," Katie said as she began to get up.

"Katie!" Margo said more firmly. Katie stopped and slowly sat back down again. "Katie, this was the third time in the last two months."

Katie turned her head away and covered her mouth with her hand.

"You saw her again, didn't you?" Margo asked.

"Yes," she said very quietly.

Margo leaned forward and touched Katie's arm. "Katie, you've got to get over this."

Katie wiped her nose again. "I know."

"How is she doing?" she asked.

"She's due in six weeks."

"Is she still hearing cases?"

"She'll stay on the job at the public defender's office until she delivers. She kept working up until the last minute with the girls."

Margo leaned forward. "I know how that must hurt, Katie."

"How could you possibly know how much it hurts, Margo? You go home every day to your son." Realizing what she had just said, Katie shook her head. "I'm so sorry, Margo. I didn't mean it like that, I'm just…"

"I know," Margo said softly. "It's okay. But there are a lot of new technologies out there…"

"The bullet ruptured my uterus, Margo. They told me I'd never be able to get pregnant."

"So you could adopt…"

"Yeah, right…an unwed ex-cop who likes the juice. I'll be a prime candidate."

"Marcus and Antoine want to," she said. "It may take a while, but they think they can adopt if they're patient. They call themselves 'Gay-by Boomers.' If they can adopt, so could you…"

"I don't know," Katie said into the distance. "It's not what I had planned. Nothing is like I had planned it," she said.

"Sometimes that's the way it is," Margo said. "You think I planned all the things that have happened in my life? Honestly, Katie, when you busted me, I thought I was history. I'll never forget the day I handed your sorry white ass that package."

Katie gave a small smile.

"A black woman carrying a bag of cocaine? You were the only one to believe that Larry set me up. You listened to me and you believed me."

"I wish she had, too."

Margo shook her head. "Katie, your sister did what she thought she had to do. She didn't believe me. You did. I'm over it. You need to get over it, too."

"She tried to get you to turn on me, Margo. She was willing to give you up to the prosecutor to put her own sister behind bars."

"She didn't know you were the one who tampered with the evidence, Katie. She thought it was someone else."

"I'm not so sure about that."

"She's your family. We don't get to choose our family. I love Marcus, but don't think it wasn't hard growing up with him fighting over every dress, every Barbie doll. You gave up your career for me, Katie, because you knew I'd lose Trevor. I know that. You believed in me and you gave me hope. I need you to believe in you and give yourself hope, too."

Katie just looked away.

FROM HER CONDOMINIUM DOWNTOWN, Alexandria leaned back in the silver chrome and mesh chair of her darkened office and watched the exchange between the two women on a large screen. Shaking her head, she reached over to shut the monitor off because she'd seen enough. Just as she was about to press the power button, the monitor flickered for a brief second and the BWA logo with the black widow spider and the red rose on its back, splashed on and off.

Alexandria blinked and sat forward. She carefully set Divinity, who was atop her shoulder, back in her glass aquarium and secured the screened cover. She tapped the space bar on the keyboard. She stared intently at the message before her:

"Still spinning webs?" it said, followed by the picture of a wasp.

Alexandria stared at it for a long time.

IT WAS VERY LATE when Katie got back to her apartment. She threw her head back against the couch and swirled the ice repeatedly around the remainder of the scotch before knocking it back. Just as she got up to go to bed, she heard a small tap on her apartment door. She swiveled the monitor that was connected to the closed-circuit camera mounted in the entryway around to face her.

He stared right into the camera.

She waited for a minute before opening the door.

He leaned very casually against the doorframe and asked, "May I come in?"

She said nothing, just stepped aside as he walked past her. She watched him carefully as he looked around the room, taking everything in, as he always did.

"I'd offer you a drink," she said, "but I really don't want to."

"I didn't come for a drink," he said.

"Then what do you want?" she asked.

"I just came to talk."

"What are you, my Rabbi again?" she asked sarcastically, referring to the police term for a trusted friend.

"Obviously not," he said.

"Then what do you want?" she asked as she folded her arms across her chest.

He stooped his tall frame down to her and said, "I came to make sure you were okay."

"What the hell do you care about whether I'm okay or not?"

He shook his head. "Look, Katie, I didn't come here to fight with you or get you all pissed off at me...again."

"Now why would I ever be pissed off at you, Joe?"

"You're always pissed off at me," he stated matter of factly.

"And why do you think that is, Joe?"

"Because you somehow have it stuck in that thick head of yours that I set you up. Katie, you've got to believe me—" he started to say as he reached for her arm.

"Believe you? Why the hell should I believe anything you say?" she said as she flung her hand away from him.

"Because I didn't give you up!" he said angrily. "I'd never do that. I care too much about you..."

"Oh, please, Joe. Spare me the 'care too much about you' crap. I suppose you want me to believe you cared so much that you weren't screwing around on me either, right?"

He grabbed her by the arm again.

"Let me go," she said as the ice in her glass spilled on the rug.

"No."

"I said let me go!" she demanded, but he was far too strong and held her tight.

"Now you listen to me, Katie Mahoney. I never denied that I broke our vows. I messed up and I'm sorry, but you want to know the truth? For a good part of our marriage, you weren't around. You were either working all those undercover assignments or when you were home, you were having your own little affair with the bottle, which apparently you haven't given up."

She felt the sting of his words. He finally let go of her as he said, "But I still loved you, even if we both made mistakes."

She stared into his green eyes.

"I swear to you, Katie, it wasn't me," he said, much quieter. He rubbed his hands through his thick black hair. "I've been trying to figure out who did it for the last three years. I don't know who it was, but if I ever find the son of a bitch, I'll kill him."

She squeezed her eyes shut.

"Katie, please, you've got to believe me," he said as he edged closer to her. She kept her eyes shut as she tried to take it all in. He reached over to brush back her hair just as he had done a million times before, but she recoiled at his touch.

"Katie, look at me," he said softly. She opened her eyes and felt her breath quicken as he reached for her again. "You know I would never hurt you," he whispered. He drew her close and gently put his arms around her. For a long time, they stayed that way. He rested his chin on the top of her head. She didn't move, didn't make him move.

She shut her eyes and nuzzled her head against his chest as he wrapped her tighter in his strong arms. Without realizing what was happening, she began to cry.

"It's okay, Katie. It's okay," he said very gently.

"I can't—" she started to say but was overcome.

"I know. It's okay," he said stroking her hair.

"I can't ever have babies," she choked out.

"I know," he said again as he pulled her even tighter. "I'm so sorry, Katie. It will be okay," he said tenderly.

She cried uncontrollably for a while. He held on to her and stroked her hair. Finally, when all the tears were gone, she wiped her eyes, cheeks, and nose and smiled up at him.

"I'm a mess," she said.

"You look beautiful," he offered.

"I look worse than when I first wake up."

He touched her cheek. "I always loved looking at you in the morning." She shook her head. "In fact, I'd like to see that again," he added gently.

She gazed up at him and offered a small nod. They retreated silently into the bedroom.

ALEXANDRIA PLACED HER FINGER in the small keypad attached to the BWA computer. The tiny device used biometric recognition to scan her finger and compare the whorls, swirls, and arcs of her fingerprint to an approved database. Every computer at the BWA had one of these devices attached to it. Passwords were too easy to crack for anyone with skill and too hard to remember for people like Jane, who balked at Alexandria's insistence that passwords be changed every two weeks. The biometric readers eliminated that problem. The system immediately powered up and the words "Good morning, Alexandria" appeared on-screen.

Katie came in. Alexandria looked over and saw the deep circles under her eyes.

"Hey," Katie said nonchalantly. "What's going on?"

"I'm examining the files from Donald Sumner's laptop."

Katie gave a small laugh. "I'm glad at least somebody is working around here."

Alexandria ignored her, but Katie remained standing by her side. Katie cleared her throat.

"Alex, about last night—" she started.

Alexandria kept staring at the screen.

"What about it?" she asked as her hands tapped away at the keys.

"I just wanted to say…thanks…you know, for watching out for me."

"I don't know what you're talking about," Alexandria said as Divinity, who was perched on the top of her shoulder, started to stir.

ALEXANDRIA SLOWLY AND VERY methodically worked her way through all the downloaded files from Donald Sumner's computer. Occasionally, Katie would meander over, but kept a safe distance because of Divinity.

"Anything good?" she asked.

Alexandria shook her head. "The usual stuff so far," she said, "although he did like to hit the porn sites."

Katie came over to have a look. "Looks more like kiddie porn to me," Katie said as she pointed to one of the girls in the picture. "She can't be more than fifteen."

THE SPECIAL FORENSIC RECOVERY software Alexandria used gave her an instant snapshot of every file that had been captured on the small, pen-like memory stick. File after file was recognized and with little effort on her own, the files were correctly matched with the appropriate software to open them up so they could be immediately retrieved and displayed.

"It looks like I've got some financial stuff here," Alexandria said. "What do you want me to do with it?"

"Put it in my folder and I'll look at it later to see if I can make any sense of it."

Just as Alexandria began to make copies of the files in Katie's folder, a small tone rang out, signaling that someone had come to the BWA entrance. Alexandria glanced at the security system monitor that automatically switched views whenever it detected motion. She stopped typing and looked at the monitor, then turned to Katie.

"What is it?" Katie asked.

Without saying a word, Alexandria swiveled the monitor around so she could see who it was. Katie gave a small sigh and said, "I'll take care of it."

"DON'T THINK YOUR SORRY white ass is welcome around here," Margo said, putting her hands on her hips, "because I've seen enough of you in the last twenty-four hours to last me a lifetime."

"The feeling is mutual, I assure you," Joe said, "but I'm here on official business."

"Official business? What kind of official business do you think you have around here?"

"I'd prefer to speak with Katie about it, if you don't mind. Is she around?"

"I'm right here," Katie said, stepping into the room. They both turned and looked at her.

"Katie, you want me to kick his ass out of here?" Margo asked, "because I will if you want."

"What are you going to do if I refuse?" he asked, "Call the cops?"

"It's okay, Margo," Katie said. "I'll handle it."

Margo looked at her curiously, but didn't budge.

"You want to call your guard dog off?" Joe asked her.

Katie bit her lip, trying not to smile.

"Who you calling a dog?" Margo demanded.

"Sorry if I offended you," Joe said with a hint of a twinkle in his eye that Katie spotted.

"What offends me is having you around," Margo said.

"Yeah? Well, the feeling is mutual," he said again, goading her on.

"You listen to me, Captain Smart White Ass, I could care less about whether you have a damn badge or a gun…"

"It's okay, Margo," Katie tried to say.

"…because you don't treat people like that…"

"Margo," Katie said again, a little more firmly. Margo stopped and looked at her. "Come on in, Joe," she said as Margo finally stepped aside. Margo mumbled something under her breath that Katie was glad she didn't quite catch.

Joe stepped around Margo, took Katie by the elbow, and said, "Can I speak to you in private?"

Katie led him into her office. She had been cleaning her gun earlier and immediately went around to her desk and shut the drawer so he could not see the assortment of badges she kept stashed in it. She watched as his eyes took everything in, including her prized poster of a shirtless Tom Selleck. Damn, she wished she'd never told him that Selleck reminded her of him. His eyes crinkled up in a smile when he spotted it. She shoved some papers aside, came back around, and sat on the edge of her old wooden desk.

"You don't need a gun or a security system with her around," he said jokingly.

"I think what Margo was trying to say was that some of our clientele might be a little disturbed to have the police show up here."

"It's not the clientele I'd be worried about," he said good-naturedly.

"We watch out for each other, that's all."

"I guess," he said.

"So what can I do for you, Joe?" she asked in a semi-professional tone. He heard the tone and gave her a curious glance. He remained standing a few feet away from her.

"I wanted you to know that I talked to Sean McCleary last night. I told him if he ever let that kind of crap happen again with the boys I'd have the liquor commission breathing down his neck so fast he'd be getting third-degree burns."

"I see," she said, running her hand across the top of her dusty desk. "That's your 'official business'?" she asked.

"No, my official business," he began as he glanced behind him to make sure the door was shut, "speaking of the liquor commission, is that I received a strange call from Samantha Steele of Sam's Saloon. By any chance do you know her?"

Katie didn't blink. "Can't say that I do."

"It seems someone came to visit her not too long ago and flashed a liquor commission badge and said they were covering Bobby O'Leary's territory." He stopped and waited. She didn't show any reaction whatsoever. "She said this person asked about a woman who might have been overserved or if someone was slipped a mickey a few months ago."

Katie stared blankly at him. He went on. "She got concerned when this person told her not to say anything to anyone and she started thinking that maybe she was going to lose her license to serve. I assured her that Bobby O'Leary, the liquor enforcement officer, hadn't switched territories and that I would look into the matter."

"And this involves me how?" Katie asked.

"Well, here's the funny thing," he began, "I asked her to describe this person, this woman who came to her bar, and when she did, I immediately thought of you, Katie."

"Really?" Katie remarked.

"Really," Joe said.

"And what did she say this person looked like?" she asked with a glint of a smile in her eyes.

"She said she had wild reddish-blonde hair, big boobs, an even bigger mouth."

Katie looked at him. "And what part of that description made you think of me, Joe?"

He moved in closer, gave her a good looking over, and slipped his arms around her waist. "Well, up until last night, I may have forgotten about one part," he said, bending forward to kiss her.

She slipped out of his arms and pulled away. "I'd be real careful if I were you, Joe."

"And why is that?"

"The female black widow occasionally kills the male and then eats him after mating."

"I'll take my chances," he said, eyeing her and smiling.

"You know as well as I do, Joe, that there are probably a thousand women in this city alone who could be described the same way."

"Yes," he said as he placed his hands on top of her thighs, "but only a few would be able to walk the walk and talk the talk."

She shrugged her shoulders. "Sorry, but I can't help you, Joe."

"Oh, but I think you can," he said as he took her face between his hands and kissed her. "In fact, you already have."

"Joe, about last night," she started to say, but he leaned forward and kissed her again. She pushed him gently away.

"About last night," she said, clearing her throat, "I…I just needed to be with someone, that's all," she said, looking away. "I don't want you to think that it meant…I don't want you to think it meant anything more than that."

"Katie," he pleaded.

"Please, Joe," she said, setting her jaw tight. "I'm not ready for this."

He didn't say anything. As he turned to leave, he said very softly, "Try to stay out of trouble, will you, Katie?"

A FEW MINUTES LATER, there was a small tap on her door.

"Come in," she said, clearing her throat.

Margo came in and gently shut the door behind her.

"Everything all right?" she asked.

"Yes," she said somewhat tersely. Then, realizing how it sounded, she said, "I'm sorry, Margo. I really am fine."

"What business does he have coming over here anyway?" Margo asked with attitude.

"It was that liquor commission thing the other day. It's not a problem."

"Katie?" Margo asked her friend.

She felt Margo's eyes on her. "He showed up at my apartment last night," she finally said.

Margo looked troubled. "Did he hurt you? Maybe we should have been watching…"

"I asked him to stay."

"You what?"

"I know, I know. All this time I assumed he was the one who gave me up, but now I'm not so sure."

"You mean you—" Margo said, her voice trailing off.

"Yes. I slept with the enemy."

ALEXANDRIA WORKED METHODICALLY AS she scoured the remaining contents of Donald Sumner's hard drive. She was almost done when she clicked on a standard operating system folder and saw an unusual subfolder named "Keep." In a subfolder below that was another folder with the name of "Save." This folder had been password protected, but Alexandria was very familiar with the password protection software, having written it herself several years ago and distributed it on the Internet for free use. She quickly bypassed it and opened up the folder.

She looked at the spreadsheets and eight image files for a few seconds but didn't understand their significance. Her curiosity was piqued as to why Donald Sumner went to such great lengths to keep these image files hidden.

Katie entered the cybercision center.

"What have you got?" she asked.

"I'm not sure. Something Donald Sumner wanted us not to see, though."

Katie studied the eight images for a few seconds before saying, "That son of a bitch."

"The reason we asked you to come here today, Amber," Katie began, "is because we've stumbled across something that we need your help in identifying." Katie nodded to Alexandria as one by one, the eight images appeared on the wall screen in front of them.

Katie watched Amber's face very carefully as recognition, then shock, set in.

"You know what these are?" Katie asked.

Amber stared at the large monitor. "Of course," she said. "Where did you get them?"

"I'd prefer not to go into that right now. Can you explain to us what they are?"

"They're body designs. The first four are for a sedan, the next three are for a sports model, and the last one is a concept car."

"And have you ever seen these before?" Katie asked.

"Of course," Amber said as she turned to look at Katie. "I designed them."

As Amber Gordon was leaving, Alexandria greeted her with the silver-covered tray. Margo wandered into the room just as Alexandria said in her monotone voice, "Would you care for a chocolate?"

146

"Yes, thank you," Amber said. Before Margo could say a word, Alexandria whipped off the lid of the silver tray. Amber Gordon's hand paused momentarily in the air before she broke into a wide smile.

"Oh, my gosh, these are so cute," she said as she took one and bit it in half.

Margo looked at Alexandria and smiled smugly at her. Alexandria seemed almost disappointed and set the tray back down.

AFTERWARD, THEY SAT AROUND the conference room dipping fresh shrimp in Margo's homemade cocktail sauce. Katie refilled her glass, sat back down, and took the platter of shrimp from Alexandria.

"I don't get it," Margo said. "Why would Donald Sumner keep Amber's designs if he didn't like any of them?"

"Because he did like them," Katie stated. Katie licked the sauce off her fingers as she passed the platter to Alexandria. "If Amber doesn't get to profit from her designs, neither should Sumner," she added.

"Meaning?" Margo asked.

"Who is Sumner Design's biggest competitor?"

"Hachi Graphics and Design in Detroit," Alexandria said.

"Send them to them."

AFTER FINISHING OFF THE shrimp, Katie, Margo, and Alexandria toyed with which one of Amber's car designs suited them best.

"I'd drive that red sports model," Katie said. "It's powerful and looks like it could take on anything and beat it."

"These days, I'd go for the sedan instead of the shitbox I'm driving now. It has room for Trevor and his friends and all their gear."

Katie turned to Alexandria. "What about you, Alex?"

"Definitely the black concept car. It's futuristic—a convergence of technology and functionality."

"Well, there you go," Katie said, "something for everyone." Just then, the screen suddenly flashed to black and for just a brief second, an image appeared, then disappeared from the screen. Alex quickly shut the power to the screen off.

"What the hell was that?" Katie asked, turning to her.

Alex sat motionless.

"What was what?" Margo asked.

"That picture. You didn't see it?"

Alexandria said nothing as Katie grabbed the remote from her and turned the big screen back on. Katie brought the images back up and scrolled through them one by one. As the end neared, she slowed the frames down. Sure enough, the same image flashed. Katie hit the "freeze frame" button.

"It looks like a bee," Margo said.

"That's not a bee," Katie said with a troubled look on her face. "That's a wasp. A mud dauber wasp, to be exact." Then she whipped around and looked at Alexandria as she said, "It's the main predator of the black widow spider."

"WHY THE HELL DIDN'T you tell me?" Katie demanded. They were sitting in her office, under the watchful eyes of Tom Selleck. Alexandria hated Katie's office with all of the clutter and heavy furniture; but in its disarray and clutter, it reminded Katie of the old police station and gave her some nostalgic comfort. At Katie's insistence, it was one of the few places at the BWA that was not covertly recorded, although Katie was never quite sure that Alex hadn't slipped a camera in somewhere. She eyed her Tom Selleck poster suspiciously.

"There was nothing to tell," Alexandria said in her monotone.

"I want to know what's going on, Alex," Katie said in an irritated voice.

"I got the first image three months ago."

"Damn it!" Katie roared. Alex remained motionless and emotionless. "Some asshole penetrated our network and you didn't tell me?"

"He hasn't penetrated our network. He's gained access to certain files, but only the ones I've allowed him access to."

"You what?"

Alexandria looked steadily at her and repeated, "He's only gotten into what I've allowed him to get into."

Katie came around from behind her desk and pulled up an old chair next to Alex.

"Alex, why in heaven's name would you have allowed anyone to access our network?"

"Because he's good," Alexandria said slowly, "…and I'm intrigued."

Katie stared at her for several minutes.

"Alex," Katie said in a much softer tone, "when you say 'intrigued,' just what do you mean by that?"

Alex folded her hands neatly in her lap. "He's good, very good. He's been able to get as far as he has with all the protections I have in place. That tells me if he really wanted to hurt or compromise us, he could have already. He's not. He's just making his presence known."

"But you don't know who he is?"

"No."

"Can you find out?"

"In time, yes."

"And you don't think he'll do us harm?"

"No."

"You're sure about that?"

Alex looked up at her. "As I said, if he wanted to do that, he could have already. I'm fairly certain of that."

"Then why is he doing it?"

Alexandria glanced briefly at the Tom Selleck poster. "I believe he's flirting with me."

15

"How's it going?" Katie asked as she paced back and forth in the cybercision center.

"Almost the same as two minutes ago when you asked," Alexandria responded with a hint of annoyance in her voice. "I'm pretty much through Sumner Design's entire network. I've created a back door entry so we will remain undetected. Because of the vulnerabilities in the latest version of the operating system that they're using, I am able to scan each individual computer. As proprietary and secure as their network is supposed to be, they've left wide open holes in it. I've been especially interested in Chester Millfield's hard drive. There were many deleted files sitting in the slack space that I was able to recover."

"It never ceases to amaze me," Katie said, "that people don't realize most deleted files are still there."

"I thought you might be particularly interested in seeing these recovered images from his hard drive," Alexandria said as she tapped a button to display them up on the big monitor.

Katie studied the photos for a minute. The two women looked at each other.

"Well, well, well," Katie said. "How very interesting, indeed."

"At least we know what his weakness is," Alexandria said.

"Are you thinking what I'm thinking?" Katie asked.

"She'll hate it."

"I know," Katie said smiling.

MARCUS CROSSED HIS LAVENDER silk-clad legs and sipped at his drink. Katie passed by him and asked, "What are you drinking now, Marcus?"

Marcus smiled. "I was so hoping someone would ask. It's Kahlúa, Irish cream, amaretto, and vodka, well shaken."

"And it's called?" Katie said taking the bait.

"A Screaming Orgasm," he said as he looked over at Antoine. Antoine smiled and raised his eyebrows at Katie.

"So tell me, Katarina darling, what is this urgent matter that you need our help on? Not that I can't say we weren't excited to help out last time, but honestly, darling, neither my Divine Miss Antoine nor I are cut out for all of this spy stuff."

Katie laughed. "It's not like that at all. We want you here for family support."

"Huh?" Margo said.

Marcus shrugged his shoulders and sipped on his drink. "How intriguing," he said. "Do explain, darling…"

As Katie explained again how Chester Millfield set up Amber Gordon, Marcus listened patiently.

"So this Chesty man dropped some Inner G in this girl's drink and that involves us how, darling?" Marcus asked.

"I won't comment on how familiar you seem to be with GHB," Katie said.

"Katarina, darling, you know as well as I do that it's the Gaytorade of the homosexual community."

"Okay, enough about that," Katie sai, rushing on. "In any case, we were able to recover some deleted images from Chester Millfield's computer and I believe we have figured out exactly how we're going to get him to make a complete confession."

She nodded toward Alexandria, who tapped a button and displayed the images on the big screen.

One by one, pictures of women in various pornographic poses appeared on screen. Every single woman was black.

Katie turned and smiled at Margo.

Margo looked at Alexandria, then back at Katie.

"What you all looking at me like that for…" Margo began to say, then stopped and shook her head. "Oh, no. No, no, no!"

"Well, gee, Margo, my sorry white ass, to quote you, would love to work this one. And Lord knows I'm good at working undercover, but even I'm not that good…"

Marcus started laughing uncontrollably.

"ALL I CAN SAY is that these had better be fifty-pound test," Margo said, struggling to get the fishnet stockings up. "And despite what you white people may think, this does not come naturally to my people," she said as she laced up the leather bustier that pushed her breasts up another three inches and strapped on the six-inch high heels.

"Push those out, Sister," Marcus said as he primped all around her. "Ah, this brings back such memories," he said, leaning back with his finger against his chin.

"You mean she dressed like this growing up?" Katie asked.

"No," Marcus said as he cinched the bustier up even tighter. "I did."

"Damn it, Marcus," his sister said, "You can squeeze and squeeze the pickle all you want, but you ain't gonna' git no cucumber juice out of it."

"She looks pretty hot to me," Katie said, walking around Margo.

"Well, well, Katie finally comes out," Marcus threw at her.

"Not quite, Marcus."

"If Mama ever sees me in this getup, she'll have a heart attack. It was bad enough her seeing Marcus."

"Then we won't mail her the photos," Katie teased.

"Katarina, darling," Marcus said as he made an adjustment, "wherever did you find this delightful HO-siery? At Sluts R Us?"

"My favorite place to shop," Katie winked.

Marcus looked over at Antoine. "Make a note of that, Antoine, in case I feel like shopping soon."

The two of them fussed over Margo and hiked the bustier up again.

"You push those things up any higher," Margo complained, "and I ain't gonna need no half-and-half for a long time coming."

"Now comes the ultimate test," Katie said. "Walk."

Margo stepped out uneasily on the six-inch stiletto heels. She wobbled and Katie caught her. "Come on, Margo, you can do it."

"Maybe he can," she said, gesturing to her brother, "but I'm not so sure."

"Sure you can, just put some attitude into it."

"It's not the damn attitude I'm worried about, Katie, it's the altitude."

"All the more reason you should have practiced with me growing up," Marcus said.

"Oh come on," Katie said. "I used to strut around in them all the time when I was working vice. I know you can do it."

Again, Margo tried to walk but she wobbled so badly that she went only a few feet and stopped.

Marcus threw his arms up. "Oh for heaven's sakes, Sister. Watch!" he said as he placed one hand on his hips and strutted up and down, hips swaying from side to side. "Now that's how a real girl walks." Margo watched him.

"Alex, what's the rule?" Katie called out to Alexandria, who was watching the whole scene with little expression.

"Ten percent acting, ninety percent attitude," she said as she stroked Divinity.

"That's right," Katie said. In unison, she and Marcus began strutting up and down the conference room snapping their fingers at each other.

"You got it, girl," Marcus called out to her.

"You've got it too, girl," Katie called back to him.

"You a bad ho," Marcus said.

"You a ho su-preme," Katie called back.

"You best be staying on your side of the street," Marcus called. "Cause I ain't sharing no business."

"Don't you be bitchin' at me, Girlfriend. Someday I be watchin' your back," Katie said, wagging her finger at him. They stopped and turned to Margo. "See?" Katie said. "It's easy. It's all about attitude."

Margo tried again.

"That's it," Katie said. "Work it. Work it, sugar. You own the street," she said.

"You the Queen Ho," Marcus called out.

"Look at that street strutter go," Katie yelled.

"I'm so proud of her," Marcus said, waving his hands in excitement.

Margo strutted back up to them both, grinning.

"And if you do a real good job," Katie said smiling, "I might just let you keep the getup overnight."

"Don't think I hadn't thought about that."

ALEXANDRIA PULLED THE VAN two blocks away from Sam's Saloon and let Margo and Katie out. They'd placed a tiny Global Positioning System or "GPS" unit earlier on Chester Mittfield's car. It indicated he'd gone from work to home and was now headed back to his favorite drinking spot.

"Remember what I told you?" Katie asked Margo.

"Safety first and foremost."

"That'a girl," Katie said. "Alex and I will be monitoring you the entire time. If you feel uncomfortable at all, just give us the signal, which is…"

"Chocolate," Margo said.

"Good. If either of us hears 'chocolate,' we'll be in there in seconds, unless of course you really dig this guy, in which case we'll see you whenever."

"Well, ain't you the funniest thing to land on this damn Earth," Margo replied.

"You never know," Katie teased her, "that's a lot of man to love…Now be careful and remember I'm right behind you. Not that I'll be able to see anything around him…"

Alex stayed in the back of the van, monitoring Margo's activities via the wireless buttonhole camera tucked in the flower in her hair.

THERE WAS LITTLE TRAFFIC in the area. Margo strolled down toward the entrance of Sam's Saloon while Katie remained hidden in the shadows. As soon as the door opened, Margo bent down and pretended to re-strap her shoe, just as Katie had instructed her. Her breasts practically fell out of the bustier and she resisted clutching at herself to get them back in. Out of the corner, she saw Chester standing in the doorway in a leather jacket, watching her. There was no mistaking who he was.

Margo turned her head away from him and whispered into her microphone, "I wonder how many damn cows gave their lives for that thing."

"HEY, SWEET SUGAR," SHE said, looking up and swaying her hips. "How you doing tonight, baby?" she asked, strutting toward him.

He looked her up and down and licked his lips as he said, "I've never seen you around here, before," in a slightly high-pitched, raspy voice.

"Then you ain't seen much," she said as she came closer. "What's your name, sugar?" she asked.

"Chester."

"Chester, I'm Candy, as in 'sweet as.' You interested in a little company tonight, Chester?" she asked as she touched his tie. He nervously looked around.

"Maybe," he said.

"Maybe you'd like a little piece of Candy to nibble on, or better yet, have Candy nibble on you?"

"How much?" he asked.

"Depends on what you're looking for, sugar," she said as she leaned forward and whispered the prices into his ear. She could see small beads of sweat form across his brow and his raspy breathing quickened.

"Do you have a room?" he asked, wiping at his shiny brow.

"Right around the corner, sugar."

Katie followed them on foot but stayed well behind as Alexandria drove ahead of them in the white van. By the time Margo and Chester got to the room, Alexandria had already slipped into the room next door and was monitoring and recording everything from the many covert cameras she had previously set up in the adjoining room. Katie was just a minute behind.

MARGO OPENED THE DOOR and Chester followed her in. Katie noticed he locked the door behind him. Margo walked over to the small bar.

"You want a drink or anything before we get down to business?" she asked. "It'll cost you a little extra."

"Good girl," Katie said.

"How about we just get down to business?" he asked. Sweat was beading up on his brow again.

"Whatever you want," Margo said as she approached the bed. Chester sat on the edge of the bed struggling to pull his jacket off, but his arms were so huge that they barely fit through the sleeves. Margo grabbed the end of his jacket and tugged. Between the two of them, they managed to get it off. Then came the shirt and the tie. By the time he was bare-chested, even Katie had trouble watching.

"I think I'm going to owe her hazardous duty pay," Katie said quietly.

"No kidding," Alexandria said.

Margo came around and kneeled behind Chester and said, "Now what was it you wanted Candy to nibble on?" she said as she rubbed his back. She looked straight at the camera hidden in the flower arrangement and grimaced.

"Extra vacation too," Katie said.

Chester dropped his pants. Katie could see the sweat dripping down his chest and back.

"Do me," he said.

"You sure that's all you want?" Margo said.

"What do you mean?" Chester asked in his raspy tone.

Margo leaned toward him and rubbed her bosom over his fat back to whisper in his ear.

"You ever been tied up while getting one, sugar?" she asked as she dangled two sets of handcuffs in front of his face.

Chester's breathing was so heavy by the time Margo secured him to the bed that she was afraid he was going to have a coronary.

"You okay, sugar?" Margo asked as she straddled him.

"Oh yeah."

"You ready to get down to business?" she asked.

"I'm ready," he said, lifting his head up and looking down just to check.

"Well sugar, if you're ready to get down to business, then so am I," she said as she inched down. Chester's corpulent chest rose and fell as he watched her intently. When she made no effort to do the job, he said, "Can we get down to business now?"

Margo folded her arms up. "You know what I'm thinking?"

He looked at her.

"I'm thinking you're such a big man, you're just too much for one woman."

Chester blinked. "What do you mean?" he said.

Margo nodded toward the adjoining room. "I have a couple of friends in there."

Chester looked at her and started breathing even heavier. "Are you serious?" he asked. He couldn't, in all of his wildest dreams, have imagined getting so lucky.

"Very serious."

"Women?" he asked just to make sure.

"Live women," she said. "Very close friends, if you know what I mean," Margo said winking at him and swaying her body slightly.

Chester licked his salty lips. Margo went to the door and flung it open. Chester watched as the two women came in. Both were completely dressed in black with leather masks covering their eyes. One was very tall and flat and one was average height and big.

"Hey girlfriends, my friend here would like to party," Margo said.

Chester tried to blink the sweat out of his eyes. Katie approached the side of the bed and sat down. "Is that right," she said as she reached into her pocket and pulled out a syringe. Chester blinked again, not quite trusting what he was seeing.

"What's that?" he asked. "I'm not into that," he said.

"Really?" Katie said as Margo and Alexandria hovered over him. "Because we heard you were."

Chester glanced between the women as his breathing grew heavier.

"What do you mean?" he said, struggling against the cuffs. He looked at Margo. "I think I changed my mind," he said.

"I don't think so," Katie said. "Not until we have a nice chat," she said as she flicked her finger against the side of the syringe to make sure there were no bubbles in it.

Chester struggled against the handcuffs, but his ample wrists, which barely fit into them in the first place, left no wiggle room. His hair was completely matted down from the sweat running off his face.

"Do you remember this room, Chester?" Katie asked, waving the needle in front of his face.

Chester blinked. "Huh? How do you know my name?"

161

"Because we know who you are and what you did to Amber Gordon," Katie said as she stood over him holding the syringe. At Amber's name, he gulped, setting off rolls of fat jiggling beneath his chin.

"I don't know what you're talking about," he lied. "Look, could you please just get me out of these?" he said. "I don't feel well."

"What do we look like, Chester, idiots?" Katie began. "You see this woman?" Katie said, pointing to Alexandria. "She just got out of jail for the attempted murder of her cheating ex-boyfriend. He's still missing certain body parts. Isn't that right, Lorena?" Alexandria nodded. "And this one?" she said, pointing toward Margo.

"This sweet little Candy is lethal. Her ex still hasn't been found." Katie leaned forward and said quietly, "She has a condition known as permanent PMS."

Margo smiled smugly. "You got that right," she said.

Chester blinked repeatedly as sweat poured into his eyes.

"Now how about you tell us why you did what you did to Amber Gordon?" Katie asked.

"I don't know what you're talking about," he lied.

"Sugar, are you always this stupid, or is today a special occasion?" Margo asked him. "You don't want to mess with her."

Katie held the hypodermic up to his face and squeezed the plunger, forcing a little fluid out of the top.

"What...what is that?" he stammered. "I'm too young to die," he begged.

"Oh don't worry, Chester, this won't kill you," Katie said.

A momentary look of relief passed by his face.

"This is a very high dose of Casitrol," she made up. "Do you know what that is?" she asked.

He shook his head "no" and perspiration flew in both directions.

"It's the chemical they use in human castration," she explained. She waited for the weight of her words to sink in. Chester's eyes grew about a foot wide as he stared at the needle.

"One dose of this and you can kiss your sweet yams bye-bye," she said as she glanced down toward Chester's huge green boxers covered in a pattern of Homer Simpsons. She brought the needle closer to his forearm. He couldn't take his eyes off of it. "Now do you want to tell us about Amber Gordon?" she asked.

"I'm telling you I don't know what you're talking about!" Chester yelled.

"Have you ever considered suing your brains for non-support?" Margo asked. "I'm telling you, she means business."

His eyes went back and forth between the three women and the needle.

"Oh God, please don't do that," he said. "Please, no!" he begged as she brought the needle closer to his arm.

"I'll give you one more chance and that's it," she said.

"They'll kill me," he screamed.

"Who will kill you?" she asked. He didn't answer.

"Just give it to him," Margo said. "I've seen bigger on a poodle anyway. No one will even notice." Chester shot her a look.

"Do it," Alexandria added with obvious enjoyment.

"No! No!" he pleaded looking at them both. "Please don't."

"You know what, Chester?" Katie said, shifting slightly on the bed. "I'm normally a very patient woman, but I don't see anything worth saving here. I could care less about your sorry little barnacles."

"I keep telling you," Margo added, "you don't want to mess with her."

"That's the truth," Alexandria said.

"So I'm not going to play around with you anymore, Chester," Katie continued. "Either you tell us about Amber Gordon right this second or you can start rehearsing for the Vienna Boys' Choir. You get what I'm saying?" she asked as she poked her fingernail into his arm.

"Ow!" he yelled, thinking it was the needle. "Okay, okay, I'll tell you!" Katie drew the needle back slightly. His breathing was very heavy and he glanced nervously at the needle again before saying, "It was the owner of the company I work for, Donald Sumner, and his son, Anthony. They wanted her out of there because she was making trouble. They had stuff to hold against me and they made me do it or they said I'd get fired. I had no choice. I never meant to hurt her. She didn't get hurt," he stupidly justified to himself. "She just lost her job."

"She didn't get hurt?" Katie asked astonished. "She lost her house, her career, and her baby," Katie corrected him.

He blinked stupidly at her. "I…I didn't think about that. I didn't know she would lose the kid, I swear. Look, I just did what they told me to do. Please, just put that thing away," he said, staring at the needle.

Katie looked at Alexandria and Margo, who both nodded. She made sure Chester was watching as she plunged the syringe, full of harmless saline solution, into her thigh and squeezed it out. His eyes widened and his mouth dropped open.

"It keeps them from growing back," Katie said, looking at him.

Chester blinked, then looked Katie up and down, first at her ample breasts and then her womanly curves. He then gave Margo and Alexandria the same once-over with a clear look of confusion in his eyes.

"Save your breath for your girlfriend," Margo hissed at him.

Chester's confidence grew. "Now will you please let me go and quit bugging me?" he asked.

Katie looked at Alexandria. "Did you hear what Chester just said? He said, 'quit bugging me.' Interesting you should choose those words, Chester," Katie said as she nodded to Alexandria.

Reaching carefully into her pocket, Alexandria gently took Divinity out of a small clear case with vent holes and placed her on the bed near Chester's face.

"Oh dear God!" he screamed. "Get that thing away from me! I told you what you wanted to know! I cooperated!"

Divinity sensed the strong vibrations he was making and started toward him.

"Please, dear God, please get it away!" he yelled as he blinked the sweat away from his eyes. Divinity edged closer to his face.

"Did you know that the tarantula prefers live prey, Chester? It loves the challenge of a kill," Katie explained.

Chester stared, horror stricken, as Divinity tentatively placed one leg on his cheek.

"What do you want from me?" Chester screamed. "I told you everything!"

"I know," Katie said, "but this is for all the women you've exploited, harrassed, and degraded."

"Oh my God, it's on my face. Jesus, get it away from me!" he said. Chester's eyes were the size of half-dollars as Divinity probed his cheek.

"Pity," Katie said with little emotion. "She doesn't like men who mistreat women, you know."

"I'll stop! I swear I'll stop," he said gritting his teeth as Divinity put another furry leg on his cheek.

"Do you think you can, Chester?" Katie asked. She glanced momentarily at Alexandria and could see Alexandria smiling behind the mask as she watched Divinity at work.

"You'd better," Katie said. "Because the next woman you mess with may not be as nice as we are." Katie stood up and twisted her body around. "You see this caboose, Chester?" she said, "You can kiss my sweet extra cars every freaking day of the week."

Chester looked perplexed and gulped. "I'll treat women better. I swear I will," he yelled. "Oh dear God!" he yelled as Divinity climbed up his cheek and headed toward his eye.

Katie nodded to Alexandria, who very slowly walked over, gently picked Divinity up, and placed her back in her pocket. Chester watched as Alexandria disappeared through the door to the adjoining room.

His face was bright red. Katie took a handcuff key out of her pocket and started to undo the handcuffs.

"Okay, Chester, here's the deal. I'm going to undo these handcuffs and you're going to be a good boy, understand? Don't even think of trying anything."

Chester nodded weakly. He looked like he'd just finished a marathon. As soon as Katie undid the cuffs, he sat up, gasped for breath, and folded his body over in his ample lap. He dropped his head between his knees and panted very loudly. Behind him, the sheets were soaked in a large, oval pool of sweat. A few minutes later, Alexandria returned with a folder in her hands.

Katie waited a few more minutes for Chester to recover. When he looked back at her she pointed to the motel door facing the street.

"Behind that door, Chester, is a police officer. You're going to tell him exactly what you just told us, do you understand?"

Bolstered by his freedom, Chester rubbed his wrists and said, "And what if I don't?"

"Then your mother will get a copy of these," Katie said as she dropped the folder on the bed next to him. He wiped his sweaty hands on the sheet as he reached for them. He stared at the glossy prints showing Margo on the bed and him in handcuffs.

He looked at the pictures with his mouth wide open, then looked up at them both and said slowly, "Who are you?"

"We're women who are tired of being exploited by the likes of you. We're women who are not going to sit around and take assholes like you mistreating us. And," she said as she strolled over to the door, "we're women who know who you are and where you live so if we ever hear about you degrading women again, we'll be back. You'd better remember that, Chester," she said as Margo and Alexandria retreated to the adjoining room. Katie opened the outside door.

Joe stood leaning against the doorframe with his jacket pulled back, exposing his gun and his badge. He stared at her masked getup.

"Having a party?" he asked. Then, leaning forward, he whispered into her ear, "Kind of brings back memories." Even with the mask on, he could see the scowl. He glanced into the room and nodded toward Chester Millfield.

"What's the deal?" he asked.

"He's ready to make a full confession," Katie said quietly to him.

"And no coercion, right?" Joe asked.

"By the book," she lied.

"I'm sure," he said with a hint of sarcasm in his voice. He looked at Chester hunched over, breathing heavily. "Is he going to make it?" Joe asked.

"Barely," Katie said. She pulled Joe aside and said, "I have one more favor to ask."

Joe gave a small sigh. "What would that be?" he asked, without even trying to hide the cynicism in his voice.

"I need twenty-four hours before you execute any warrants."

Joe shook his head. "Oh, come on, Katie, you know we're not supposed to sit on a warrant like that."

"I know," Katie said, "but you're a captain now. You can do this stuff. Just lose the paperwork or find a typo in it or something, but give me twenty-four hours to tie up a few loose ends."

He studied her for a moment, looked back over at Chester, then nodded. Katie stepped aside and let him in.

"Okay, lover boy," Joe said, "it's time for you to get dressed and take a ride downtown."

THEY WENT BACK TO the office for a debriefing.

"Casitrol?" Margo asked as she brought out a container of homemade chocolate-"Obviously not," he said. hip ice cream from the freezer while still in her undercover getup.

"I almost accidentally said 'castor oil'." Katie laughed as she grabbed three bowls.

Margo watched her and smiled. "Does this mean you're joining us in the celebration?" she asked.

Katie grinned. "All chocolate, no calories," they said in unison.

"He still would have been petrified," Alexandria added as she grabbed the hot fudge sauce and can of whipped cream.

"That boy's ass looked like two pigs wrestlin' over a Milk Dud," Margo said. "Looked like he was sweatin' Crisco or something," she added as she piled scoops of chocolate ice cream into their bowls. Margo warmed the hot fudge up in the microwave.

"I wish you could have been on my side of the bed to see the look on his face when I shot the saline into my leg," Margo said as she poured the warmed hot fudge sauce over the ice cream. It steamed slightly. She shook the whipped cream can and mounded it up in circles. Then she grabbed a sharp knife out of the drawer, along with a bag of walnuts. She poured the walnuts out onto the cutting board, held the knife up in the air, and said, "Here's to Chester's nuts," as she brought the blade down. They all cracked up.

"Nice touch with Divinity," Katie said to Alexandria. "I'm not sure which terrified him more, the thought of becoming Chesiree or Divinity crawling around his face."

Alexandria smiled like a proud parent. Katie raised her bowl and said, "Here's to yet another successful Black Widow mission." They raised their bowls in unison to salute, but as they glanced at each other, their smiles disappeared. They all put their bowls back down.

"It doesn't feel quite right, does it?" Katie said quietly as she looked at them.

"I admit it. I miss her and her damned hot flashes," Margo said.

"Me too," Alexandria said very quietly. Katie and Margo looked at each other with shocked expressions on their faces.

LATER, MARGO, WHO STILL hadn't had a chance to change out of her costume, reached over to put the last clean bowl away in the cabinet. Katie came up from behind her and playfully goosed her.

"Go on, Margo, get out of here. I'll finish up."

"You sure?"

"We'll catch up on everything in the morning," Katie said.

"I'll just run inside and change," Margo said, looking down at herself.

"You give new meaning to the words 'ho-maker,'" Katie teased. "Why don't you bring it back in the morning?" she said. "Unless, of course, you're too tired."

Margo grabbed her cell phone and made two calls. Marcus and Antoine, who wanted to adopt a child of their own, were more than happy to keep Trevor for the night. Cal said he'd be right over, wondering what the big surprise was…

16

KATIE WALKED INTO THE BWA kitchen and stopped in the doorway. "Jesus, Mary, and Joseph," she said with a slight trace of her mother's brogue. "What the hell is that smell?" she asked, covering her nose and fanning the air in front of her.

Margo had rubber gloves on and was wiping down the trashcan while Alexandria sprayed the air with deodorizers.

"Dead fish," Alexandria said.

"Old shrimp, actually," Margo said, correcting her in a slightly annoyed tone. "Somebody was supposed to take out the damn trash, but forgot," she said as she glared at Alexandria.

"No one asked me to do that," Alexandria said.

"Maybe you would have remembered better if I sent you an e-mail instead of actually asking you to your face," Margo snapped back. "You're on that damn computer so much, you're ass is gonna go digital…"

"Okay, okay, enough," Katie said as she covered her nose. "I've smelled cadavers that weren't that bad," she said. "Just get that stuff

171

out of here before we have to evacuate the building. When you're done, meet me in the conference room."

MARGO PLOPPED DOWN IN a chair in the conference room and tried to stifle yet another yawn.

"Looks like someone spent too much time in bed, but didn't get enough sleep last night," Katie teased.

Margo grinned. "Sorry," she said.

"That's okay," Katie assured her. "Did you and Cal…"

Margo smiled. "All night long, but don't worry, I'm having that professionally cleaned."

"Too much information," Katie cautioned her.

Alex came in and sat down.

"Is it ready?" Katie asked.

Alexandria nodded.

"How bad is it?" Katie asked.

"Bad," Alexandria replied as she let Divinity perch on her knee.

The three women watched the big screen as the video from Sumner Design played. The small, car-shaped computer mice had worked out perfectly, capturing clear audio and video. Alexandria had already edited and spliced the digital movie down to ten minutes.

They watched in near silence as a young man with black hair wearing a Sumner Design identification badge sat back in his chair and downloaded a pornographic video from the Internet called "Pillage and Plunder," of a young woman being raped by two men. Soon, several others, including the silver-haired Donald Sumner, meandered over to watch. The audio was clear enough to make out the vile words as each man cheered the action on and described in detail what they would do to her. Just then, the young red-headed receptionist, Doreen, passed by to ask Donald Sumner to sign a form. The angle of the hidden camera on the computer mouse showed as one by one, they grabbed her as she tried to move away.

"You love to get it like that, don't you?" the dark-haired young man asked.

"Maybe you'd like to get it from us all," another said.

Donald Sumner smiled, looked almost right into the camera, and said, "Maybe you'd like to get it from the boss, first."

THEY SHUT THE VIDEO off and shook their heads. For a while, none of them could speak.

"Somebody needs to smack those boys up the side of the head a few times," Margo finally said. "They never heard of sexual harassment laws?"

"Nothing's changed," Katie said. "Despite changes in the law, sexual harassment is pervasive across this nation. Even the federally funded National Institute of Health just got in trouble recently for a case. It happens covertly, overtly, inconsistently sometimes, but it's still very much out there." She looked back up at the screen. "It's just usually not that bad, but Sumner Design is a privately owned business so there's no overseeing board of directors, no watchdogs to make sure it doesn't happen. Even if there were, it doesn't guarantee it still wouldn't happen. It was pervasive in the police department, but we all just sucked it up and figured that was the price we paid for trying to break into a male-dominated field. Policies were issued whether they were always adhered to or not."

"That poor girl," Margo said. "She must hate coming to work every day."

"I'm sure she does, but she needs the paycheck and that annual bonus just as bad. I bet she has a kid or two at home that she's trying to support, so she just puts up with it." Katie sighed. "Hopefully, that's about as bad as it ever gets," Katie said pensively. "I just wish I could figure out what to do with it…"

A voice from the doorway said, "Send it to Davis Venture Capital." They all spun around.

"I'll be damned!" Margo said leaping to her feet and giving Jane a hug.

Katie held back, but rose from her chair.

"Hello, Janie," Katie said quietly. Margo stepped back.

Jane nodded.

"You want to come in and sit down?" Katie asked.

Jane shook her head. "I have something I want to say," she began.

"Alex and I can go make some fresh coffee," Margo said discreetly, but Jane stopped her.

"It's okay, Margo, I want you all to hear this." She turned back to Katie. "I've been thinking a lot about the things we talked about, Katie. I realized sitting at home playing with the cat and organizing picture albums of MaryJane wasn't going to make much of a difference in anyone's life and I know you've made a difference in each of ours," she said as she looked from Margo to Alexandria. "I'm not saying I agree with how everything is done around here, but I suppose sometimes it's necessary to get the job done, as long as it helps someone."

Katie nodded. "Does this mean you're back on the team, Janie?" she asked. They waited anxiously for Jane to respond.

"Yes," she said with a small amount of hesitation. "That is, if you'll have me back."

Katie smiled and nodded. "You were never off of the job as far as I was concerned," she said stepping forward and hugging Jane. "Besides," she said nodding toward Alexandria. "It was getting kind of chilly in here. We need someone to crank up the heat."

"I can certainly do that," Jane said, fanning herself.

"Hello, Alexandria," Jane said, eyeing Divinity perched on Alexandria's knee.

"Hello," Alexandria said quietly back as she picked Divinity up and cradled her in the palm of her hand.

Jane sniffed the air. "No offense, but what is that awful smell?"

"We've been invaded by some bad shrimp," Katie explained. "Hopefully it will go away soon. Tell me you won't change your mind because of it?"

Jane looked at her and smiled. "I'm a lot tougher than that, Katie," she said.

"I know you are," Katie said, placing her arm on Jane's.

"Besides," Jane said, "if I don't stay, the whole thing would have been an awful waste…"

Katie looked at her confused. "What whole thing would have been an awful waste?" she asked.

"This," Jane said as she pulled up her pant leg. They all stared in disbelief at the small black widow spider tattoo complete with a red rose on Jane's inner right ankle.

JANE EAGERLY BIT INTO a chocolate spider as they passed the tray around. She threw her head back and said, "I missed these so much."

"Don't worry," Margo said, "I've been eating enough of them to make up for you while you were gone."

"So who are these people you want us to send the video to?" Katie asked as she licked the chocolate off of her fingers.

"Davis Venture Capital. According to the files you sent me…"

Katie knew full well that she hadn't sent any files to Jane. She looked over at Alexandria. Alexandria just gave her a small smile and shrugged.

"…Davis Venture Capital is on the verge of making a significant investment in Sumner Design in return for a guaranteed share of the company because they think Sumner Design is far more solvent than they really are. Sumner Design is maintaining two sets of books. The financials on Donald Sumner's laptop showed they're in much deeper trouble than even I imagined. I guarantee you, if Davis Venture Capital sees this video, they'll pull out so fast…"

"Other than not investing in Sumner Design, do you think they'll do anything else with it? Send it to the media, for example?"

"Not likely. They're used to companies having skeletons in their closet and I'm sure strict non-disclosure forms have been signed, so I doubt they'd do that."

Katie sat and thought for a moment. "Alex, can you get into Donald Sumner's schedule and see everything he's going to be doing in the next twenty-four hours?"

Alexandria brought up an e-mail calendar and switched to day mode, then zoomed in.

They all saw it at the same time.

"It can't be," Katie said as they all stared at her. "Hang on a minute," Katie said as she got up and grabbed her purse. She rummaged through it until she found the folded-up green flyer. She hadn't bothered to look at it before but now the Sumner Design logo was right there along with "Proud sponsors of the Shamrock Shores Assisted Living Facility."

"I'll be damned," Margo said.

"Janie, when we were checking out this place for my mom, I asked you to look into them, remember?"

"Yes, but I…"

"No, no, Janie," Katie said quickly, "I'm not accusing you, besides, the name wouldn't have meant anything to any of us at that time. All I want to know is if Sumner Design should suddenly pull its sponsorship, will the place survive?"

"Yes, they were funded primarily through a group of physicians. Sumner Design's contribution is minor."

"Why would an auto parts designer invest in an old people's home?" Margo asked. "Doesn't make sense to me."

Katie shook her head. "I don't know, but I imagine we'll find out. What time is it?"

"Eight thirty-two."

Katie turned to Alex. "That means we only have three and a half hours. Alex, how quickly can you edit that video so the female employee of Sumner Design is not visible?"

"I'd need an hour."

"That's all you've got. She's been victimized enough and I don't want her to be victimized again. Okay, Margo, I want you to contact the media. Tell them that there's going to be a huge surprise at the Shamrock Shores Grand Opening. Tell them you're with the

177

White House if you have to, no…wait, better yet, tell them you're calling from Hollywood. That will get more attention. Tell them you're an agent for…Tom Selleck and that his aunt is living there and he's going to make a surprise appearance. Make sure they send a video camera crew."

"Tom Selleck? What is it with you white people all in love with Tom Selleck?"

"Margo…" Katie said.

"Okay, okay. I'll do it."

"Janie," Katie continued, "I want you to go back to the second set of books, the real books, and put together a very simple spreadsheet showing the true net earnings of Sumner Design, not what they've publicly distributed. Keep it simple, but make multiple copies of that along with their phony financials and we'll all help to assemble them in a binder. Alex, as soon as you've cleaned up the video, burn a bunch of copies and we'll add that to the binder as well. We've got to get this information into the hands of the media."

"I'll get right on it," Jane said.

"Ladies, the black widows have hung upside down spinning webs for long enough. It's time now to eat our prey."

17

"You're sure this will work?" Katie asked.

"They're using a wireless remote connection, which I've already hooked into," Alex said from the back of the van. Katie looked over and saw several news trucks pulling up.

Katie turned to Jane. "You have the CDs for distribution?" she asked. Jane showed her the stack of CDs with "The Real Story Behind Sumner Design" on the label. The Sumner Design logo appeared on each one.

"Nice touch on the logo," she said. "Okay, you and Margo stand by for distribution. She turned back to Alex. "On my signal, Alex," she said. Alexandria nodded.

Katie looked at her watch, jumped out, and went up to the green front doors of Shamrock Shores. There were green balloons everywhere. She quickly worked her way through the crowd of bystanders, some of whom waved to her, to get to the auditorium. She scanned the crowd and spotted her mother. Timothy Collins was seated on one side of her. Her sister, Kelly, was on the other.

Katie glanced up toward the small stage and saw the silver-haired figure of Donald Sumner leaning over to speak to the mayor. Edwina Sumner stood by his side, chatting with Gracelyn MacDougal. Katie worked her way through the residents and dignitaries and squatted down beside her mother.

"Katie!" her mother said, squeezing her hand. "I never expected to see you here."

"I can see that," Katie teased as she said hello to Timothy Collins. He politely shifted over one seat and offered Katie his chair. Kelly leaned forward and said, "Hello, Katie."

Katie nodded her way. Her sister looked very uncomfortable and rubbed her hand on her belly.

"I'm so glad you came," Molly Mahoney said, as she touched her daughter's cheek. "This is going to be quite the show. They even have some big presentation planned," she sai, pointing to the screen.

"Oh, it will be a show all right," Katie said quietly.

Kelly looked around at all the media setting up. "I'm surprised at all this press coverage," she said, leaning forward to Katie. "Whoever handles their PR is doing a great job."

"Is that Tom Selleck?" Katie heard someone call out as she glanced toward the back of the room. With his dark sunglasses on, Joe could almost pull it off. He stood quietly as some of the reporters rushed over to him. Kelly and her mother turned around and, realizing who it was, looked back at her curiously.

"How nice of Joe to come," Molly Mahoney said quickly.

"I have a feeling he's here on official business, Mom," Katie explained. Kelly looked at her and raised her eyebrows.

Katie smiled and glanced up just as Edwina Sumner, who looked like she was dying for a cigarette, scanned the audience. Katie watched curiously as Edwina Sumner spotted her and seemed to lock eyes with her. Donald Sumner also paused to glance at the audience, and there was no mistaking the look of recognition as his eyes came to her. Just then, Gracelyn MacDougal rose and approached the podium.

The crowd became silent.

"Ladies and gentlemen, I want to welcome each and every one of you to the Grand Opening Celebration of Shamrock Shores, Laketon's newest and finest assisted-living community." Everyone applauded. "I know many of you are excited about the luncheon buffet we've planned afterwards, but before we begin the festivities, I'd like to introduce someone very special who is here to make a presentation today."

Katie smiled.

"As you know, without our corporate sponsors, we would never have been able to build this wonderful facility. It is with great pleasure that I introduce a friend of our community, Mr. Donald Sumner, president of Sumner Design."

The audience applauded as the silver-haired man took the stage. Edwina Sumner stood off to his right in her Chanel suit and turned to listen to her husband speak.

"'Tis a fine day, indeed, lads and lasses," Donald Sumner said in a poor attempt at an Irish brogue. The audience laughed politely. His eyes scanned down to the row where Katie was sitting. He cleared his throat. "Seriously, folks, this project has been an absolute joy. Sumner Design is delighted to be a part of this community and to help our neighbors out. Isn't that right, honey?" he said, motioning for Edwina to join him. Edwina smiled and came over. He put his arm around her as he said, "I'll warn you fellas out there that this gorgeous gal is already spoken for." The audience laughed again. "Now, I'm sure many of you are unfamiliar with who we are and what we do, so we've put together a very short presentation to explain what the Sumner Design family is all about…"

Katie picked up her cell phone. "Now," she said very quietly. Her mother was completely absorbed in the presentation on stage, but her sister leaned forward, having heard Katie, and tried to get her attention. Katie put the phone away.

Donald Sumner aimed the remote at a portable multimedia projector connected to a laptop and hit "play."

Smiling, he stepped back, keeping his arm around his wife's waist as the video began to play.

THE AUDIENCE WATCHED AS the Sumner Design logo swirled around the screen, then dissolved into an office setting whereby a group of men, one whose silver-hair was quite recognizable, stood around a computer monitor. A buzz rose in the audience when they realized exactly what was playing on the computer monitor.

Donald Sumner's mouth dropped open when he realized it as well. On the big screen, the young red-headed woman whose face had been completely blurred, struggled to get out of the arms of the men.

"You love to get it like that, don't you?" the dark-haired man wearing his clearly identifiable Sumner Design ID badge asked.

"Maybe you'd like to get it from us all," another one said.

"Maybe you'd like to get it from the boss, first," Donald Sumner said on the big screen.

CHAOS ENSUED AS THE press surged forward, shoving cameras and microphones in the face of Donald Sumner. Gracelyn MacDougal ran up to the podium and yelled, "Ladies and gentlemen, please remain seated and stay calm."

Katie watched as Edwina Sumner stiffened her back and pulled away from the arm of her husband.

"Edwina," he said, "I can explain. It's a joke. Someone's playing a joke," he pleaded.

"Mr. Sumner," a reporter yelled, "are you aware that just minutes ago, your son was arrested for conspiracy to commit second-degree assault and possession of a controlled substance?"

Edwina Sumner put her hand to her mouth. Katie watched curiously as Gracelyn MacDougal rushed over and put her arm around Edwina Sumner. It was then that Katie noticed the resemblance between the two women.

"This is all a mistake," Donald Sumner said loudly. "It's all a mistake."

Katie glanced toward the door as Joe pushed his way through the press. He wore a sports coat, but the badge and gun were clearly visible. Two uniformed officers followed him. He shoved through the crowd, announcing "Police" several times. When he finally got through, he stopped, fully aware of all the cameras.

"Mr. Donald Sumner?" he said.

"Yes, thank God," he said in a relieved tone. "There's been a terrible mistake here, Officer. I don't know what's going on," Donald Sumner pleaded.

"That's Captain, and what's going on, sir," Joe began as he reached behind for his handcuffs, "is that you are under arrest for fraud, simple assault, and conspiracy to commit second-degree assault."

Katie focused on the expression on Edwina's face as her mouth dropped open. "Call the attorneys!" Donald Sumner shouted at her. "Call them right away."

Edwina Sumner gathered herself up, looked right at him, and said, "I'll be calling the attorneys all right, to file for a divorce!"

As Joe slapped the cuffs on him, a reporter held up a red folder, which Katie recognized from having helped assemble several sets of copies earlier back at the office. The reporter called out, "Mr. Sumner, is it true that you've been maintaining two sets of financial records?" Donald Sumner looked out as the reporter waved the red binder at him.

"No comment," he mumbled.

"Mr. Sumner," another one said, flipping through the pages of the binder, "is it true that you set your own daughter-in-law up to be arrested by injecting her with drugs and then planting them on her?"

Donald Sumner looked pleadingly at Joe to get him out of there.

"Mr. Sumner," a female reporter yelled, "how long has this kind of sexual harassment been going on at your company?" she asked with a tone of vengeance in her voice.

Donald Sumner looked like he was about to faint.

It occurred to Katie that Joe was taking his own sweet time getting him out of there. She could have kissed him for that.

Kelly Mahoney leaned forward toward her sister. "Interesting turn of events," she said.

"Isn't it though?" Katie asked smugly.

AMBER GORDON SAT IN the conference room chair across from Katie.

"And Chester made a full confession?" she asked, astounded.

"Let's just say the truth was sweated out of him," Katie said.

"I couldn't believe it when I saw the whole thing on the news," Amber said. "My phone was ringing off the wall. I had reporters calling me all day and night."

"It isn't often that a major corporation gets caught with its pants down, if you know what I mean."

"So what happens now?" Amber asked.

"You'll need to file a motion for a new hearing to have the charges dismissed."

Amber dropped her head down and sighed. "I don't have any money to hire an attorney," she said.

"I know," Katie said just as a very pregnant woman with the same color hair and eyes as she walked through the door. "Amber, meet my sister, Kelly, the legal eagle of the downtrodden."

The two women shook hands and Kelly slowly lowered herself down into the chair. The two sisters said nothing to each other.

"Katie's filled me in on your situation," Kelly began, "and with Mr. Millfield's confession and all of the charges being filed, I don't see any reason why your conviction shouldn't be overturned. In conjunction with that, we'll request that all charges be expunged from your record. Unfortunately, we can't erase people's memories, but that's as good as it gets and with all the publicity, your story will be told."

"And my daughter?" Amber asked right away. "Will I get Vanessa back?"

Kelly glanced at Katie for just a second, then turned back to Amber.

"Yes, but there's a process to all of this, so you'll need to be very patient. The charges your ex-husband and ex-father-in-law are being arraigned on are very serious felony charges. I will file an emergency petition requesting that custody of your daughter be given back to you, at least on a temporary basis…"

"Temporary basis?" Amber asked alarmed.

"Temporary until we can get the case overturned," Kelly explained, "then I'll file for a motion for reconsideration for custody. Realistically, I don't see any reason why you shouldn't get permanent full custody back."

Amber's face lit up. "I don't believe it," she said. "It's like a miracle."

Kelly leaned forward and handed Amber a card. "This is my information. Call me later today."

Amber Gordon stood up and shook hands with Kelly.

"Thank you so much," she said sincerely.

THE TWO SISTERS SAT across from each other.

"I appreciate you taking this on, Kel," Katie said.

"I still don't know how you did it," Kelly said.

"How I did what?" Katie asked innocently.

"You know exactly what I mean, Katie. The confession, the double set of books, the videotape. And I have a good idea some of it wasn't done using legal methods."

Katie studied her sister. "Oh come on, Kelly," she said, "you know as well as I do that sometimes the scales of justice get tipped. You've seen enough of your clients get hung for stuff they didn't do to know that," she added.

Kelly nodded. "True," she said, "but I still prefer to work within the limits and confines of the law."

"To each his own," Katie said.

"Yes," Kelly said, "as long as I don't end up having to represent you someday."

"Represent me? I figured you'd prefer to prosecute me."

Kelly sighed. "Katie, are you ever going to let that go?"

"You know what, Kel? It's hard to forget when your own family turns on you."

"I didn't turn on you. I didn't know you were the one to take the drugs out of evidence, Katie. I thought it was…"

Katie waited for her to finish. "You thought it was who?"

"Joe."

"He was your brother-in-law."

"And the two of you were already on the outs. Look, Katie, I thought it would help you. I swear that's the only reason why I encouraged Margo to turn and give someone up."

"They offered her a deal and you told her to take it."

"She was facing a lot of jail time, Katie. The case was solid and I thought it would help her to take the plea and give up what she knew. I just didn't expect her to…"

"To what?" Katie asked. "Refuse to cooperate? You would have let an innocent woman, a young mother, go to jail for a long time for something she didn't do."

"Her story was shaky. The case was black and white."

"As in a black woman carrying white powder."

"How dare you judge me like that, Katie. You seem to forget that I'm the one who says 'innocent until proven guilty'."

"If you had taken the time to talk to her, to get to know her, you would have realized she wasn't capable of trafficking drugs. She loved her son too much. If I hadn't…done that, her life would have been ruined because you didn't believe her when she said she was innocent."

"You forget that most of my clients walk in and say they're innocent. And I'm the one trying to get them off."

"But you were so sure she was guilty."

"What do you want me to say, Katie, that I messed up? Okay, I messed up. I see thousands of cases a year and none were as rock solid as hers. The case was built around your undercover work, Katie. She had the dope on her when you arrested her. The case was based on your report, so don't blame this all on me. The evidence was solid. That's why I encouraged her to cooperate with the prosecution. But I swear to you that I didn't know you were the one to tamper with the evidence. Believe me or not, but it's the truth."

Her sister sighed and very slowly eased herself out of the chair using both arms to push herself up.

Katie weighed everything Kelly had just said before asking, "You going to make it?"

"We're Mahoneys," Kelly said, "we'll all make it."

18

THE FOUR WOMEN SAT on bar stools around the Black Widow Agency kitchen and watched, absolutely transfixed, as Margo explained the traditional celebratory cake in detail.

"This is called a chocolate genoise cake, which is named after Genoa, Italy, its place of origin. It's different from a regular sponge cake because of the melted, unsalted butter that gets added to the batter. That makes it light and airy and a little less sweet than regular sponge cake." Margo looked up and saw the gaze on all three women's faces, smiled, and continued on. "The cake is sliced in half and layered with a chocolate mousse filling, then a white chocolate mousse filling made of mascarpone cheese. That's all chilled, then covered in a silky fudge frosting."

Margo picked up her pastry bag and squeezed out decorative mounds of fresh whipped cream all around the top of the cake. She delicately placed strawberries on the top of each whipped cream mound. They all leaned in a little farther as she stirred the small pot of melted dark chocolate on the double boiler. Dipping a long pastry knife in it, she drew it out quickly and drizzled the melted dark chocolate across the top of the cake in a zigzag pattern.

She stepped back and turned her head to the side, studying her work. Then she slowly looked at the three women and one by one they looked at each other and grinned.

"Ready?" she asked.

They all drew their hands out from their laps to display their forks.

Katie shut her eyes to fully enjoy the taste. "You know what they say," she offered, "Coffee, chocolate, men…Some things are just better rich." She gestured toward the cake with her fork. "And this definitely qualifies."

A FEW WEEKS LATER, Katie staggered into the conference room fresh from a run. Margo clipped the stems of lilies, watching Katie wince as she hobbled toward the bar.

"You okay?" Margo asked.

"This healthy lifestyle is going to kill me," Katie said.

"I don't know what you're bustin' your ass for, Katie. Me, I got on the digital scale this morning and it read, 'One at a time please,' but you don't see me running around like a damn fool."

"Thanks for the support," Katie scowled.

Alexandria, as usual, was engrossed in her ever-present laptop. Jane pored over the latest pictures of her granddaughter.

"Look, she's got my smile, don't you think?"

"Aha," they collectively groaned.

Antoine studied fabric samples and kept laying them out side by side on the table, then swapping them against each other. Marcus sat back casually and sipped on his oversized cocktail. Katie caught a whiff of Marcus' drink as she passed by.

Instinctively, she asked, "What you got there, Marcus?" Immediately, Margo began to wave at her in silence from behind Marcus' seat. Margo put a finger to her throat and made a slicing motion. Katie frowned at her and ignored her. Margo nodded her head toward Jane just as Jane looked up. Margo threw her hands up in a defeated gesture.

"It's a lovely combination of amaretto, melon liqueur, rum, Southern Comfort, and vodka."

Katie watched as Margo shook her head and nudged it again in Jane's direction, but Katie couldn't resist. "And it's called?" she asked as Margo rolled her eyes.

Marcus savored the moment, took another sip, and peered at Antoine before slowly responding, "An Anal Penetrator."

Jane looked up and her mouth dropped open. She immediately blushed.

Marcus and Antoine grinned at each other and Marcus rubbed the top of his hand on Antoine's knee.

"Come along, darling," he said, taking Antoine's hand. "I think this drink is getting to my head," he said dryly.

Katie burst out laughing.

"You gone blonde or what?" Margo finally said. "You don't get what this—" she repeated the throat-cutting gesture, "—means?"

Katie shrugged innocently. "I thought you had an itch," she said. Margo shook her head.

Jane stood up and passed a magazine to Katie.

"I thought you might be interested in this," Jane said.

Katie looked at the high-gloss magazine.

"Wow," she said.

Margo came over to see what it was. The real estate magazine featured a full-page ad with multiple pictures of a gorgeous house.

"Now that's a house," Margo commented.

"That's Amber Gordon's house," Jane said.

Margo looked down at the asking price and gulped. "Sweet Jesus," she whistled. "And here I'm still asking for a price check at the Dollar Store. Someone's gonna make a damn fortune."

"That someone," Katie said, "will be Anthony Sumner. Amber lost all claim to the house in the divorce proceedings."

"And how is that fair?" Margo asked.

"It's not fair, but it's the law, unfortunately," Katie said. "He had the better attorney," she added. "By that point, Amber could barely afford to hire an attorney."

"But that's the house she poured her heart and soul into building," Margo said.

"It does seem a shame she can't get it back," Jane said.

Katie chewed the inside of her cheek as she thought about that. She looked again at the asking price. "She can't get it back at that asking price," Jane said.

"So this asshole Anthony will make all the profit off of her design?" Margo asked, shaking her head.

"Unfortunately," Katie said.

"Well, that stinks," Margo said. Katie whipped around and looked at her.

"What you lookin' at, girl?" Margo asked, wondering why Katie was staring at her.

Katie looked at Jane when she said, "Nothing."

Margo pressed her. "Oh, no, Katie. I can see there's something swirling around in that frizzy head of yours."

"I was thinking about one thing," Katie said, "but…" She broke off and drifted away. Margo and Alexandria turned to Jane and stared at her with expectant expressions on their faces.

"Oh for heaven's sake," Jane said, "would you all please stop staring at me like that?" she said as she fanned herself. "Katie, if you think there's a way to help her out…"

Margo patted Jane on the shoulder. "That'a girl, Jane," she said. "One of these days, I just know you're gonna kick ass."

"Actually, it was you who gave me the idea," Katie said.

Margo raised her eyebrows skeptically. "Huh?"

"Well, if you've got a good plan," Jane said, "it doesn't matter who came up with it. Just spill it."

"That's the thing," Katie started, "I was trying to think of a good plan, but as Margo pointed out, 'the whole thing stinks.'"

19

KATIE AND MARGO RODE in the back of the "Divinity Interiors" van with Jane and Alex up front. Katie stopped Margo before she opened the door.

"You have everything?" Katie asked.

Margo reached into her tool bag and took out the large bag filled with fresh shrimp. "Armed and dangerous," she said.

"Okay, we'll have to work very quickly. Janie? Alex?"

Each woman produced their own respective bags.

Katie glanced one more time at the blueprints of the house that Amber had supplied to them. Katie's explanation that they might someday want to build a new headquarters of the Black Widow Agency seemed odd, but Amber was so grateful to the women for having gotten her daughter back to her, she would have given them blueprints of the moon had they asked for them.

Katie looked at all the red circled points. "Everyone knows where they're going?"

"Conservatory, dining room," Jane answered.

"Living room, family room," Alex said.

"Upstairs bedrooms and office," Margo said.

"And I'll take the bathrooms and be on the lookout," Katie said. "As always, the safety word is 'chocolate.' If anyone hears 'chocolate,' we abort the mission. Understood?"

"Y'all start yelling 'Chocolate' at me, I'm gonna need to stop and eat," Margo said.

"All right then, sound check," Katie said. "Testing one, two, three."

Everyone acknowledged receipt of the signal.

"Okay, ladies," Katie said. "May the power of the Black Widow Spiders be with you all," she said half-jokingly.

They jumped out of the van and strolled up to meet Antoine and Marcus at their black BMW.

"What took you so long, darlings?" Marcus asked impatiently. "Were you all shooting up estrogen or something back there?"

Katie glanced back at Jane. "Now there's one idea we never thought of," she said.

Everyone started walking toward the house. Even from the road, the women were awestruck at the house. It was an oversized and expanded cape, but not overly domineering because of the use of natural materials. The façade was covered in a combination of native fieldstone and cedar shingles, including a massive fieldstone fireplace and a welcoming front porch. Balancing the main part of the house were two rounded, full-height rooms of cedar shingle with floor to ceiling glass. One was used as a family room, the other as a conservatory.

Katie, who knew very little about houses, nevertheless whistled.

"It's gorgeous," Jane said.

"Damn, it's beautiful," Margo said. "I can't wait to see the inside."

"Nice," Alex said, looking up.

"I MAY DECIDE TO buy it for real," Marcus said as he approached the house. "What a lovely little nest to raise birdies in," he said to Antoine.

"You can't," Katie cautioned him. "That's not part of the plan."

Marcus threw his head back. "Katarina, darling, it will pain me to see something so gorgeous and not have it because you do know how I love gorgeous things," he said, reaching out and taking Antoine's hand.

They all strolled up to the front of the house with Marcus and Antoine in the lead. The door opened before they had a chance to ring the bell. A blonde woman in a tight gold suit swung open the door.

"Welcome," she said, and then upon seeing Marcus and Antoine holding hands, she said, "Oh my..." She quickly recovered and put out her hand. "I'm Karen Warren of Prime Properties."

Marcus took her hand and kissed it. "*Enchantee*," he said. "I'm Marcus and this is Antoine." Antoine shook her hand.

Karen Warren stiffened slightly. "You're the 'couple' here to view the house?"

"Isn't that what was discussed on the phone?" Marcus asked. Marcus looked back at Margo, who had made the call to set up the appointment.

"Yes, but I just thought—" Karen Warren began.

Marcus edged a little closer to Karen Warren as he said, "That we'd be white?"

"No…yes…I mean no, of course not," Karen Warren stammered. Realizing her gaffe, she quickly added, "It's just that this is a very…traditional neighborhood, you know."

"Of course it is, darling," Marcus said. "And we're here to make our own traditions," Marcus said.

Katie could see Margo's clenched fists and gently touched her on the arm and shook her head slightly. Margo nodded back but Katie could tell she was furious.

"I have another couple coming to see the house in a little while," Karen Warren lied, "so if you don't mind, we'll need to look at it quickly."

"Really?" Marcus challenged her. "But I thought we would have at least an hour. Isn't that what was arranged?"

Karen Warren said glibly, "There must be some confusion then. I do have others waiting to view the property."

Marcus turned back to Katie and gave her a small shrug. "Very well then. Ladies, come along."

Karen Warren stepped forward to stop them. "I don't understand," she said. "Who are all these people?" she demanded.

"These darling girls are part of our team," Marcus explained. "They're here to make sure all of our antiques will fit. Antoine and I have a number of prized possessions and they must all fit. Our lovely team members are just going to take a few measurements in some of the rooms while you show us the house."

"I see, but Mr.—?"

"Marcus."

"Mr. Marcus, this is highly unusual."

"Karen, darling," Marcus said, "this is a highly unusual property. Everything must fit. Now come along, I want you to give us the grand tour. Don't leave a single detail out. Antoine, sweetie," Marcus said, "you did bring the checkbook, didn't you?"

"I'm afraid I can't just let these…girls…wander around unsupervised," Karen Warren said, putting her hand to her hip.

"It's women," a voice rang out from the back. They all turned to look at Jane, who shoved her way to the front. Katie could see the beads of sweat forming on her forehead and the rise in color from her neck up.

"I beg your pardon," Karen Warren said, somewhat affronted.

"No offense taken," Jane said, "but perhaps you should contact your manager or whoever supervises you and explain to them how you wouldn't allow the staff of Sachet and Sashay, one of the premier interior design teams in the entire Northeast, to take a few simple measurements."

They all stood staring at Jane for a few seconds. She wiped her hand on her brow and retreated back. Margo gave her a small squeeze on her arm as she passed by.

"Did you say 'Sachet and Sashay'?" Karen Warren asked with immediate recognition. "You're that Marcus and Antoine?" she asked.

"The one and only," Marcus said with a slight bow.

"Oh, Mr. Marcus," Karen Warren said, "I just sold one of the houses you redid on Tremont."

"That would have been the Delaney's," Marcus added for clarification.

"Yes, it was lovely."

"That's right, darling," Marcus said, "so now why don't you stop wasting everyone's time and show us this lovely hunk of real estate."

"Of course, Mr. Marcus," Karen Warren said as she swept her arms around the house. "With pleasure. Would you like to start in the kitchen?"

"Of course," Marcus said with just a hint of sarcasm in his voice. "Measure everything, my little Killer Bees," Marcus said as the women assembled their ladders, clipboards, and pencils.

As soon as they were out of earshot, Margo turned to Jane and hugged her.

"Wow," Katie said, "now that was a power surge."

"I'm so sorry, Katie. I don't know what happened," Jane said, fanning herself. "I…I just couldn't help myself."

"Thank God for that," Katie said.

"That white woman's so stupid," Margo added. "I bet she stares all morning at the orange juice box just because it says 'concentrate'."

THEY BEGAN IN THE conservatory, the spacious room with curved walls and floor to ceiling glass. Even Katie, who knew nothing about architecture or interior design, was impressed. She looked over and could tell that Margo was just about wetting her pants.

"Damn, it's gorgeous," Margo said as she took in the entire space.

"Come on, Margo, there'll be time for looking later," Katie gently said.

They pulled the bags out of their pockets. Katie climbed the ladder by the first curtain rod, unscrewed the end cap, and tucked as many shrimp in the open rod as she could. Room by room, they found places to tuck the shrimp into: in the doorbell chime cover, in the wall mount of the light sconce, behind the switch plates. The shrimp were very fresh and didn't smell…yet.

"They're coming to the dining room," Katie called out as everyone shifted positions. "They're headed upstairs," she said a few minutes later. Eventually, she heard Marcus and Antoine coming back down into the foyer.

"I'm as excited as the day I met Liza," Marcus said. "Isn't it divine?" he asked Antoine. Antoine smiled and said, "Absolutely."

"Oh, there you are, darlings," Marcus said. "How did we do?"

"Everything will fit perfectly," Katie said.

Marcus smiled. "Excellent," he said.

Karen Warren rubbed her hands together. "We could write up a contract right now," she said.

"Wonderful, darling," Marcus said, "as long as we have the appropriate contingencies in place."

"Of course," Karen Warren said with dollar signs practically reflecting in her eyes. "I've got the paperwork in the den." She rushed out and returned. "What kind of contingencies were you looking for?"

Marcus eyed the four women. "We'd like a three-day clause to withdraw from the offer pending house inspection and approval."

"Absolutely," Karen Warren said. "Not a problem. You're very lucky because it's a very hot property."

"Let's hope so," Katie said quietly.

Prior to leaving each room, Alex had bypassed the heating system, using the detailed instructions from Amber Gordon, and turned each thermostat up to maximum temperature. Then she changed the password on the thermostat system so it could not be reset.

Karen Warren could not understand why the house was so hot when she went back to gather her paperwork the following day. She also couldn't tell where the odd odor was coming from. On the third day, she agreed to meet Marcus and Antoine at the house to finalize the contract. They were there early and waited for her to open up the house. Karen opened the front door and they all recoiled.

"Mother of Mercy," Marcus yelled. "What in the world is that?" he said, covering his nose with Antoine's jacket. Antoine pulled away.

"I'm not sure, Mr. Marcus. Perhaps an animal got inside or something."

"An animal?" Marcus asked. "It smells like an entire zoo may have succumbed in there, darling."

"I'm sure we can find out what it is. Let me just open some windows to air it out." Marcus and Antoine were amazed as Karen Warren sucked it up and walked back into the house and began opening windows. She looked a bit green when she reemerged. It helped only mildly.

"It appears the thermostat is stuck. I'll have it looked at," she said.

"Darling, you can have the thermostat looked at, but it's not the heat that I object to," Marcus said as he stood at the threshold of the door scrunching up his nose.

"I'll get a professional cleaning crew in here. Trust me," she said desperately, "it will be all right in a day or two. We'll extend the contract," she said in a pleading tone.

But it wasn't all right in a day or two. It got worse. Much worse. Prime Properties hired a professional cleaning crew who cleaned the house from one end to another, but still the smell lingered. To Karen Warren's frustration and disappointment, Marcus and Antoine withdrew their offer. Day after day, Karen Warren came two hours prior to any showing, opened every window and sprayed the house from one end to the other with heavily scented floral spray, but it didn't help. The odor lingered on and prospective buyer after prospective buyer pulled out. The price plummeted. Finally, Karen Warren got a call from a woman named Donna Dormond who worked for a mortgage broker. She said she represented a small, private holding company named "Divinity Capital" and was looking for real estate investments in the area. Her clients were prepared to make a cash offer, sight unseen. The price they offered was one-third the original asking price. Karen Warren faxed the contract over immediately.

20

AMBER GORDON BOUNCED HER little girl, Vanessa, in her lap. "I can't ever begin to thank you for all you did," she said to Katie, tears welling up. "I still can't believe everything that happened and that I have this back, too," she said gesturing around the large glass conservatory.

"It's a gorgeous house," Katie offered.

"Thank you," Amber said, "but no one has been able to explain to me why it sold so cheaply or how this holding company was able to defer the mortgage payments like that."

"It's a new program," Katie explained. "It's meant for single moms like yourselves who just need a little extra time to get back on their feet. You know, sort of like a student loan."

"And all of the charges have been dropped and I have full custody of Vanessa," Amber said, kissing the top of her daughter's head. "Now all I need is a job so I can start making payments."

Katie reached into her pocket. "Maybe this will help," she said as she passed an envelope over. Katie watched as her mouth fell open upon opening the envelope.

"What is this?" she asked astounded.

"It's a check for your body designs from Hachi Graphics and Design. Apparently there are still some honest companies out there and when they received your designs, they wanted to compensate you for them so that they could hold the legal rights to them. There are some papers you'll need to sign before you can cash that check. They'll fax them over first thing on Monday."

"I don't know what to say," Amber said with tears again welling up in her eyes.

Katie reached out and touched Vanessa's hair. "Tell your mommy it's okay. She deserves it." The baby smiled and cooed. "They're also very interested in seeing any additional designs you might have and discussing a possible position at the company," Katie added.

"This is all too much. I'd love to show them more designs," Amber began, "but they're based in Chicago and my family is here in the Northeast." She looked down at Vanessa. "And right now, I don't think I'm in a position to move."

"I know," Katie said. "It's just something for you to think about and in the meantime, that check should hold you over for a bit. I'm afraid there won't be any money coming out of Sumner Design. I don't know if you've heard the news or not, but they've folded. Declared bankruptcy. It seems they were in far worse shape than anyone knew and with the recent publicity the manufacturers have all pulled their contracts, citing violation of federal sexual harassment laws. Their manufacturing and corporate buildings are on the market as we speak."

"So everyone is out of a job?" Amber asked.

"Unfortunately," Katie said, "but the women who worked there have gotten quite a bit of attention since things came to light and as I understand it, most of them have been offered positions with other local businesses. Several women-owned businesses have specifically come forward and offered them jobs."

"That's a relief," Amber said. "Maybe you could get me the names of those companies and I could apply too?" she said half-jokingly.

"Funny you should mention that," Katie said as she glanced at her watch.

Just then, the doorbell rang. Amber Gordon got up to answer it but Katie stopped her. "Why don't you let me get that," Katie said. "I have a feeling I know who it is."

Amber looked very curiously at her and sat back down.

Katie walked back in a minute later followed by an older woman dressed in a fitted tan silk suit.

"Amber Gordon, this is Mrs. Gloria Duvay, an acquaintance of mine."

"How do you do," Gloria said as the two women shook hands. Gloria gently patted Vanessa's head and sat down next to Katie. "My husband and I happened to be driving through Hyde Park the other day looking at properties," Gloria began, "when we stumbled across your house. Richard was intrigued by it. He loved the design and structure and wanted to know who the architect was. Knowing Katie was familiar with the area, I asked if she could find out. Coincidentally, she said she knew you."

Katie smiled at Gloria's rehearsed speech.

"Gloria's husband," Katie explained, "is Richard Duvay, the president of Du-Tech Architectural Designs."

"I'm flattered," Amber said humbly.

Gloria turned and winked at Katie before turning back to Amber. "Richard was so impressed, he'd like you to come in and speak with him about a position he has open on his design team."

Both women watched as Amber's eyes got very wide.

"But I'm not licensed," Amber said.

"Oh, that doesn't matter. They have plenty of architects on staff who can sign off on the final plans. That's not what Richard is looking for anyway," Gloria explained. "He prefers someone who is not a product of architectural schools. He likes fresh, unadulterated ideas. He would rather work with someone with a non-traditional background who hasn't been 'molded' by the standard thinking of architectural colleges. Your design was, in his words, 'invigorating.'"

"That is," Katie interjected, "if you can stand to design houses instead of cars."

"Yes," Amber said immediately. "Yes, I'd love that."

Katie stood up. "In that case, I'll leave you two ladies alone to work out the details."

Amber Gordon stopped Katie and gave her a big hug.

"I don't know what to say," Amber began. "You've done so much for me. You've...you've given me back my life."

Katie smiled, patted Vanessa's head, and then gently squeezed Amber's arm. "And someday I may just ask you to return the favor," she said as she turned and began to walk away.

"I'd love to see the rest of the house," Katie heard Gloria say as she reached the door.

THE FOUR WOMEN GATHERED at the kitchen of the Black Widow Agency to sample Margo's latest creation—chocolate-orange Pots de Crème with a candied orange peel. They salivated while waiting patiently for Margo to present them each with their dish.

"To Amber Gordon getting her life back and staying strong," Katie said, raising her bowl.

"You know what they say," Margo said, "a woman is like a tea bag…you don't know how strong she is until you put her in some damn hot water."

They all laughed.

"To Donald Sumner for leaving his laptop behind," Alex said quietly as she raised her bowl.

"And to everything falling into place," Jane added.

Katie lowered her bowl with a strange look in her eyes.

"What's the matter?" Margo asked. "I've got more in the refrigerator, don't worry."

"No, it's not that," Katie said. "It's what you said, Jane. Everything did fall into place." The women looked at her curiously.

"So?" Margo asked.

"It all fell into place too easily," Katie said as she put her bowl and spoon down. She got up. They watched her as she grabbed her purse.

"Where the hell are you going now?" Margo yelled as Katie headed toward the door.

"To find out why!" she yelled over her shoulder.

THERE WAS NO RESPONSE from the doorbell, so Katie walked around the expansive yard and spied her sitting out back on a lounge chair by the pool. A young, deeply tanned and very muscular young man wearing only shorts leaned forward to light her cigarette. Katie watched as she touched him affectionately on the shoulders and said something that made him smile. Katie opened the gate and without invitation, walked in.

Edwina watched from behind her Chanel sunglasses and took a long drag from her cigarette. After taking a slow sip from her drink, she gestured for Katie to sit down. Both women turned and watched the young man as he dragged a long hose around the pool.

"Gives new meaning to the words 'water sports,'" Katie said.

Edwina ignored her, but kept watching the young man. Finally, she turned to Katie and asked, "Would you like a drink, Miss Mahoney? Carl makes a wonderful margarita," she added as she licked the salted lip of her glass.

Katie sat down. "I'm all set," she said. "I see you know who I am…"

Edwina Sumner turned and watched Carl bend over to pull leaves out of the pool with a long rake. "It must be so nice to be young and carefree," Edwina said. "Maybe now I'll get to enjoy more carefree things."

Katie watched her carefully, unsure which tack to take.

"How long have you known about all this?" Katie asked.

"About what?" Edwina asked innocently.

Katie just stared at her, refusing to play into the games.

"Oh all right," Edwina finally relented. "It took me a little while to recognize you at that grand opening," she said, "but you look exactly like the picture in that article," Edwina said, glancing quickly at Katie's ample bosom.

Katie remembered the one and only photograph she had allowed to be taken of herself for an article on the agency when they first opened. The staged picture was of Katie in a low-cut sweater leaning over a monitor with the headline "The Black Widow Agency—Digital Bytes You'll Never Recover From." They subsequently used the headline as their agency logo. Katie took a lot of good-natured teasing about it from everyone she knew. The guys at the department all wanted to know what she was willing to bite. She thought the article's shelf life had expired, but with archived files available on the Internet, apparently it hadn't.

"So you knew," Katie said.

"I wouldn't have even thought of it except that the article stated you shared office space with Marcus and Antoine. I happened to stumble across the article right when I hired them. I called my sister to confirm everything."

"Gracelyn MacDougal."

"Yes. Gracelyn was the one who talked Donald into investing in Shamrock Shores."

Katie tapped the table, considering all of this.

Edwina continued. "Of course I almost believed Marcus when he called and gave me that story about a new magazine wanting to do an article on my house, but then when he told me the editor's name, it sounded very familiar so I looked up the article and it was almost the exact same name…"

Katie bit her lip. She had forgotten that Alex's name, as well as the others', had all been mentioned in the article.

"So then I knew. When Marcus suggested she see Donald's office, I was certain."

Katie thought about all of this as Edwina sipped her margarita smugly.

"You're sure you won't join me?" Edwina asked again, alternating between sips and puffs.

Katie shook her head again. "So you set your husband up," she said casually.

Edwina turned to her. "You wanted what was on the laptop and you got it," she said coolly.

"You knew that's where the damaging files would be."

"Of course."

"Still, you took quite a chance," Katie observed.

"Some things are worth the risk," Edwina said, stabbing the air with her cigarette. The trails of smoke drifted toward Katie.

"And what do you get out of it? Sumner Design declared bankruptcy. All of their assets and equipment were seized."

Edwina laughed sardonically. "Sumner Design falls under corporate protection. They couldn't touch Donald's personal assets." She made a sweeping gesture with her arm. "And Donald had plenty of personal assets, despite what little cash flow the company had."

"Despite or because of?" Katie suggested.

Edwina smiled.

"Donald paid close attention to all of the Fortune 500 executives who ended up being investigated by the federal government and were left with nothing but the clothes on their back. So yes, for the last few years he had siphoned off what he felt was 'adequate compensation' and quietly paid himself in cash, which was then reinvested. Now all of it is mine. Donald can kiss his assets good-bye."

Katie watched her. "But your son—" she said. The change in Edwina's expression was immediate.

"I did not mean for my son to be caught up in all this!" Edwina said sharply. Recovering, she added, "You may find this hard to believe, Miss Mahoney, but I did not know what Anthony did to Amber. I am truly disappointed about all of that." She took another sip from her margarita.

"If you don't mind my asking, why did you wait so long to do anything about it?" Katie said.

Edwina gestured toward her. "Are you married?"

"Divorced."

"So you know that all marriages have good times and bad."

Katie nodded.

"Donald and I had many good times in the beginning," Edwina said. "Watching him build up his business was exciting. This may come as quite a surprise to you, Miss Mahoney, but I was well aware of what was happening in my husband's company. The few times I would go there to drop things off…well, let's just say I'm not blind. Then there were the affairs. At first he was discreet, but toward the end he made no effort to hide them." She glanced at Carl as he pulled leaves from a rake. "I got tired of him having all the fun. It's my turn now, and now I can have it all. Under the terms of the divorce settlement, I will be taken care of financially. The house is mine. I have medical insurance and a monthly income that is more than sufficient. And most of all, I'll have my freedom from thirty-eight years of him lying to me, watching him flirt with every woman in his sight, and the embarrassment of it all. Do you know how happy that makes me?" she asked. "But I am truly sorry that Anthony got caught up in all of it, too."

Katie shook her head. "Have you spoken with him? With Anthony?"

Edwina looked at her steadily. "I have. They've both hired a competent attorney who thinks they can bargain, you know what I mean…"

"Plea bargain," Katie offered.

"Yes, plea bargain the case so it does not have to go to trial."

Katie stood up because there was nothing left to say. Edwina pointed toward her with the cigarette. "Perhaps someday Amber will thank me," she said.

Katie stopped short and turned back to her. "Thank you? Do you have any idea what that woman went through losing her only child?" she asked.

"As a matter of fact, I do," Edwina said, and with that, she turned her head away in a dismissive gesture.

22

JANE LANDERS SAT IN her parlor, putting the newest pictures of her granddaughter into a picture frame while sipping on a glass of iced tea. Her cat, Angel, popped up on her lap just as a cool breeze blew in unexpectedly through the open windows. Jane put her head back to let the refreshing breeze cross her hot skin. For the first time she could remember in the longest time, she felt cool.

"It's wonderful, isn't it?" a voice called from the screened door.

Jane jumped up, spilling the cat to the ground. "Oh, Mrs. Mahoney," she said as she opened the door.

"It's Molly, please," she began as she extended her hand. "I almost didn't want to disturb you, you looked so content."

"I was looking at pictures of my granddaughter, MaryJane. But it's been a while since I actually felt cool. Please, do come in."

"Tell me about it," Molly answered sympathetically. "I slept naked as a bird for almost five years trying to stay cool."

"She's beautiful," Molly said, picking up the picture of the baby with red hair. "They are such fun."

"I just wish I saw her more often. They're down in Boston."

"That's not that far."

"I know, but they're…busy quite a bit."

"These young people all seem to have busy lives, don't they? I'm fortunate to have my girls so close, even still…"

"I don't think that's what you came here to chat about, now is it?" Jane asked.

"I escaped the clutches of Shamrock Shores for a wee bit because Katie asked me to have a chat with you about all you're going through, if you don't mind. You know our Katie, she sometimes sticks her nose where it doesn't belong, so if you'd prefer me to go, I won't be offended in the least."

"Don't be silly," Jane said, "I'd love to chat. Would you like to join me in a cup of tea?" she asked. "Or perhaps you'd prefer something stronger?"

"How strong are we talking?" Molly Mahoney asked with a twinkle in her eye…

ACROSS TOWN, MARGO PULLED a light sweater over her tank top as a cool breeze filled the air. She sat on a large quilt and opened up a picnic basket filled with a walnut salad with warm bacon dressing, crispy deep-fried chicken, deviled eggs, fresh strawberries dusted with powdered sugar, and a rich chocolate mousse cake, and began to set everything out on the old heirloom quilt. After opening a bottle of chilled wine, she looked up and saw Cal chasing Trevor, as Trevor ran away at full-speed with a football tucked under his arm. Margo smiled and waved to them both.

IN THE DARKENED CORNER of her office, Alexandria stroked Divinity's back and sipped on a diet soda while she waited for the screen to reappear. The wasp image appeared out of nowhere and she quickly set Divinity back in her cage as she turned back to the screen.

"Hey, Spider Woman," the note said, "do you want to play a game?"

She recognized the line from the movie *War Games*, in which a young man inadvertently hacked into a government computer, nearly setting off World War III.

"What game did you have in mind?" Alex responded.

"Have you ever heard of 'The Mating Game'?" it said.

Alexandria gave a small smile.

"I like to know who I'm playing with," she said as her hands flew across the keyboard. Within seconds, a video screen popped up of a man about her age with long, dark hair pulled back in a ponytail and a goatee. He was smiling as he waved to the camera.

"What's your name?" Alexandria said as she enabled her own video camera. She waved back.

"Derek," he wrote, "but my friends call me 'Dark Hunter.'"

"You know who I am?" she typed.

"Yes. You're the renowned 'Geek Goddess.' Fascinating, mysterious, intelligent, and very beautiful, if you don't mind my saying so."

Alexandria smiled shyly.

KATIE JOGGED ALONG THE banks of the Potoc River that paralleled Laketon's downtown waterfront. The entire loop was three and a

217

half miles. Struggling to finish the last half mile, she pushed forward. She suddenly felt a vibration coming from inside her hooded gray sweatshirt and pulled out her cell phone. She glanced at the caller ID before flipping it open.

"Speak to me," she said between breaths.

"I'm the one with the best view by far."

She glanced around and saw Joe running up quickly from behind.

"And that's the only view you'll get," she said as she shut the phone and picked up her pace. His long legs made it easy for him to close the gap between them. With all the effort she could muster, she made it to the end of the river two strides ahead of him. They both doubled over, out of breath.

"We're not twenty-five anymore," Joe said as he caught his breath.

"Speak for yourself, Joe," Katie said panting. "I was doing fine."

KATIE SAT ON A bench overlooking the river while Joe slipped into a nearby café and bought them two bottles of iced tea. She noted the brick buildings on the opposite shore, all once working mills that had since been converted to high-priced condominiums. At least the river remained unspoiled. A blue heron dove into the water and came out with a small fish that it eagerly devoured. Katie watched as a young mother pointed the heron out to her small child. The little boy waved his arms wildly at the bird, but the heron did not budge.

"Cheers," Joe said as they clinked bottles.

"That bird isn't going to move," Katie observed as the young boy got closer to it, flapping his arms and waving them up and down.

"Why should he? He's hungry and he has his food. I wouldn't move either," Joe said, patting his stomach.

Katie kept watching the young boy.

"Katie?" Joe said softly. When she didn't respond, he reached over and patted her leg. "Katie?" he called again.

"Do you ever think about it, Joe?" she asked.

He knew very well what she was asking.

"Sure."

"Don't you ever wonder why?"

"Why what?"

"Why it happened."

"Katie…"

"I need to know, Joe. Somebody took a part of my life away from me and I need to know why." She slowly turned to him but he averted his glance. She saw the expression of confusion on his face. "You know, don't you?"

Joe sighed and ran his hands through his hair. "Katie, what difference does it make now?"

"What difference does it make?" she asked in an incredulous tone. "What difference does it make?"

"I mean what's done is done. What good will it do to dredge it all up again?"

"I need to know," she said in a throttled tone. "I have the right to know, Joe."

"Katie, you always said you were a career woman, anyway. We never discussed having kids and I accepted that."

219

"I said that, Joe. It doesn't mean I meant it. Don't you think I thought about it? Every woman thinks about it." She shifted on the bench and faced him. "I want to know, Joe."

Joe uncrossed his long legs and dropped his clasped hands between them. With his head down, she could see the sprinkling of gray hair throughout his head.

"Maybe we should go somewhere else to talk about this."

"I want to talk about it here and now."

He resigned himself to this and sat up. "I'm sorry, Katie."

She studied his face and tried to understand what he was saying. "Sorry for what?"

He shook his head. "It was my fault."

"I don't understand."

He rubbed his hands through his hair again. "Chelsea Mattox."

Katie soured at the mention of the name.

"What does a junior police reporter have to do with my getting shot?"

Joe gulped. "I told her you were working undercover. Katie, I never meant to, I swear to you. She kept asking me why you were never around. I told her you were on special assignment, but I'm sure she figured it out."

"Why would she care where I was?" Katie asked. The look on Joe's face told her why.

"By the time she and I...You had already filed for divorce, Katie. I'm sorry."

Katie waited a few minutes before saying, "I want to know everything, Joe."

"She was jealous. She knew that even though you and I barely spoke, that we still had something special. We always did, Katie, and it drove her crazy. She threatened to tell you about us, but I told her to take a hike. But she didn't go to you. Instead, she snooped around and found out what cases you were working. She had a lot of street contacts. She got to someone and blew your cover."

"When did you find this out?"

"A few weeks ago. I never stopped trying to find out, Katie. I know how much getting shot changed your life. I just didn't have all the pieces until a few weeks ago when I talked to the shooter, Wykoff. He was up for parole, so I decided to put a little pressure on him to see how badly he wanted to get out. He said Chelsea Mattox approached him with an idea for a piece on the 'desperate world of drug traffickers,' and promised him it would all be kept anonymous. She dropped your name and described you well enough that there was no question in Wykoff's mind who you were."

"And now?"

"The statute of limitations has run out, Katie, or I'd charge her with everything I could. Even at that, it would be a convicted felon's word against a locally known reporter's. Katie, I can't tell you how sorry I am…"

WITHOUT A WORD, KATIE stood up and walked away.

"Katie, wait!" Joe yelled as he tried to grab her by the arm. She struggled and broke free. "Katie, I'm so sorry. You have to believe me," he pleaded, but his words were lost to the wind that had suddenly picked up. She broke away and ran toward her car, tears streaming down her face.

The blue heron, sensing the change in the wind, took flight.

LATER THAT EVENING, KATIE searched among the many customers in the downtown cyber café. She found Alexandria sitting at a small table with her back against the wall, thereby obscuring the screen of her laptop from anyone else's view. Katie felt her cell phone vibrate for the sixth time and knew it was Joe. Once again, she ignored it, and slipped into the chair next to Alexandria.

"How safe are we here?" she asked.

"I'm browsing on a public wi-fi wireless account that would be traceable back to the café only. There are no records of access kept and I can pass through several anonymizers so they'll be no trace whatsoever."

"Good."

Katie reached into her pocket and took out a slip of paper with a name on it. Alexandria recognized the name immediately and looked at Katie.

"A woman?" she asked quietly.

"Yes."

"But I thought…"

"Forget about what you thought. The black widow spider will prey on a female when necessary."

"You're sure?"

"Call it a gut instinct, but yes."

Alexandria nodded. "What do you want done?"

THE END

If you enjoyed *The Black Widow Agency*, read on for an excerpt from the next book by Felicia Donovan.

Spun Tales

COMING JULY 2008 FROM MIDNIGHT INK

ONE

"Ready, Alex?" Katie Mahoney asked Alexandria Axelrod as she handed her a black leather briefcase. Alexandria nodded. "You're sure about this?" Katie asked with some hesitation. "You know you don't have to do it. I can just tail him all the way."

"It's fine."

"And the bailout word is?"

"Chocolate."

"If either of us has any problems or even if something doesn't feel right, that's the emergency word. And if either of us has any emergency cravings, that's the solution," Katie added laughing.

Alexandria gazed at her vacantly.

"Remember, the only thing I need is the room number," Katie said as she glanced out the one-way window toward the street. Suddenly, a heavyset, middle-aged man with gray hair and thick, tortoise-shelled glasses came into view.

"Okay, it's showtime."

Katie pointed the video camera out the window of the white van that had "Divinity Florals" painted on its side. "That's him," she said pointing, "navy-blue suit, white shirt, floral tie, gray hair, Coke-bottom glasses." She motioned Alexandria to come over so she could see her target. Without thinking, Katie touched Alexandria's elbow to pull her closer. Alexandria immediately recoiled.

"Sorry," Katie said casually. "You see him?" Alexandria nodded. "Wait… wait… okay, go."

Katie sat back and watched as Alexandria, with her long legs and wide stride, easily caught up to the man and fell into step behind him as he approached the entrance to the Constitution Hotel on Bolton Avenue. This was a routine case; although she knew from her years as a police officer that there was danger in letting one's guard down and feeling complacent. Still, all the wife wanted was the incriminating evidence before she filed for divorce and so far, it had been an easy case to work, the husband having enjoyed the company of one of the new assistants routinely every Tuesday at two PM. All they needed now was the video to finalize the case and they could wrap things up and start on the next one.

BUSINESS WAS BOOMING AT the Black Widow Agency, where disgruntled wives and girlfriends hired Katie and her co-workers to get the goods on their errant husbands and boyfriends. When they weren't in the field using the latest covert video surveillance cameras, they were back at the offices using the latest computer forensic software to digitally analyze amorous e-mails, recover deleted e-mail orders for flowers and trinkets, and uncover undisclosed bank accounts. It was hard work and long hours, but the women of the agency, all of whom had been scorned in one way or another by a man, were more than up for the task, especially if it meant helping a woman in need.

KATIE SWIVELED THE MOUNTED chair and switched to the remote cameras and microphones located in the briefcase Alexandria was carrying. She watched and listened on her headset as Alexandria, without giving the man so much as a glance, stepped into the elevator behind him. He turned around and politely asked her what floor she needed him to press. Alexandria deliberately fumbled around in her purse until she saw him press "six."

"Sixth floor, please," she said, pulling out her cell phone and taking a few discrete pictures of the man while they rode up. As the elevator doors opened, the man stepped aside to let her exit first. Alexandria stepped out of the elevator and fumbled around again in her purse for a small compact. With her back to the man, she pretended to freshen up her lipstick. She pressed the small lid release in the front of the compact; a mini camera zoomed in, giving Alexandria a clear shot of the hallway directly behind her. She noted the door the man knocked on and could hear a woman's voice as it was opened. With her back still toward him, Alexandria captured the woman embracing the man and drawing him in. As soon as the door was shut, Alexandria removed her shoes, tiptoed down the hall, noted the room number, and headed down the stairwell.

Upon hearing three successive raps on the van's back door, Katie opened it and held out her hand to help Alexandria up, but Alexandria ignored the gesture and grabbed onto the door to hoist herself up.

"Six-twenty-two," Alexandria announced as Katie jotted down the room number on a "Divinity Florals" receipt.

"Wish me luck," Katie said as she grabbed the gift basket that Margo Norton, their office manager, had assembled for them earlier. In it were Lindt chocolate truffles, a bottle of champagne, glasses, and some imported cheese and crackers. Woven throughout the basket were tiny remote buttonhole cameras disguised as the heads of flowers.

Katie pulled her "Divinity Florals" cap down low on her head and without saying another word, hopped out the back of the van. She walked into the main lobby of the hotel with a confident stride, as if she went there every day. The concierge looked up briefly at her. Katie smiled and waved to the young man as if they'd met many times before and held up the basket. He nodded toward her and waved back. Without a word, she stepped onto the elevator and rode up to the sixth floor.

She knocked on the door and waited.

"Who is it?" a man's voice called out.

"Delivery," she said loudly. She deliberately smiled at the peephole and held the basket up in front of her.

The man opened the door just a crack. His tie was off, his shirt was half-unbuttoned, and his belt was loosened. Katie glanced behind him and saw a young woman on the bed wrapped only in a hotel robe.

"Delivery," Katie said again and without asking, tried to push past him and walk in.

The hefty man positioned himself in the doorframe and put his arm out to stop her as he pushed his thick glasses back up on the bridge of his nose. "There must be some mistake," he said, "we didn't call for any delivery."

Katie frowned and showed him the receipt. "Constitution Hotel, room six-twenty-two." The man took the receipt from her and studied it.

"What is it, Saul?" the young woman sitting on the bed asked.

"I'll take care of it," he said, glancing nervously over his shoulder. He pointed to the receipt and showed Katie. "It says 'Harrington,'" he said. "You must have the wrong person," he added as he handed her back the receipt.

Katie pretended to study the receipt more closely, then glanced at her watch.

"Oh shit. They must have already checked out. Damn!" she said, glancing nervously back and forth. "Look, I'm going to catch all kinds of crap if I bring this back to the shop," she said. "I was supposed to be here for this morning but that damned traffic… Do me a favor would you and just keep it anyway, okay?"

"But we didn't—" the man started to say, but the young woman with the long, dark hair sauntered up behind him and placed her hand on his shoulder. She was half his age and not altogether attractive. Her nose was a bit too large for her face and her hair was a variation of colors from auburn at the roots to brunette at the tips, as if she couldn't quite decide what color she wanted it to be. She was well-endowed and the robe was open enough for Katie to see her biggest assets.

"Ooh, is that champagne?" the young woman asked in a nasally tone as she leaned closer. She slipped her arms around the man's waist and oozed out, "I wouldn't mind a little champagne before we…"

The man glanced nervously at Katie and back out the door. "Okay, whatever, we'll keep it."

Katie shoved past him and set the basket on the dresser directly in front of the bed. "You two have a real good time," she called out over her shoulder as she strolled back down toward the elevator.

"LET'S SEE WHAT'S ON our favorite channel," Katie said as she took a seat in the back of the van. Alexandria was already at the console monitoring several views from the cameras.

"That's the most expensive gift basket they'll ever get," Katie said, referring to the cost of the hidden cameras. The view was incredible. "Excellent video quality."

"Those are the VT-twenty-threes," Alexandria explained with some pride. "They have three hundred and eighty lines of resolution, a point five low lux rating, the latest CMOS imager, and a built-in three-point-five millimeter lens with a sixty degree field of view."

"Let's just hope his wife appreciates the fine quality of the video," Katie said as she watched the woman undo the man's belt.

"Looks like he has a sweet spot," Katie chuckled. Alexandria watched with no expression whatsoever on her face. "Or should I say," Katie corrected herself, "a sweet and low spot." She leaned back a bit as the sordid action began to unfold in front of her. A few minutes later, she commented, "If that's him all worked up, there sure doesn't look like there's much to work with." Katie rocked the chair back and forth and the two women watched in silence for several minutes.

"Is it just me," Alexandria said after a few minutes, "or does it look like he's swaying?"

Just as she uttered the words, they watched on the monitors as the man slumped forward on top of the young woman, forcing her back onto the bed by his body weight. Katie and Alexandria glanced at each other for a second in disbelief, then back to the monitor as they watched the young woman struggle to climb out from under the collapsed body.

"Oh, boy," Katie said as she grabbed her cell phone and dialed the office of the Black Widow Agency.

"What are you doing?" Alexandria asked.

Margo Norton answered the phone immediately. "Hey, Margo, it's Katie."

"How's the action?" Margo asked. "You learning anything new, Girlfriend?"

"Yeah, that sex can kill."

"Huh?"

"Listen, I need you to get on an untraceable line right away and call 9-1-1 for a possible heart attack at the Constitution Hotel, room six-twenty-two. Got that?"

"Constitution Hotel, room six-twenty-two," Margo repeated back. "Got it."

They continued to watch the video monitor as the young woman finally managed to extricate herself from underneath the body. She shook the man repeatedly and called his name. He didn't move. The young woman picked up the hotel phone, held it in the air for a second, then quickly set it back down.

Katie and Alexandria watched in shock as the young woman gathered up her clothes, slipped her dress back on, and stole out of the room, leaving her fallen lover to fend for himself.

"Nice," Katie said, shaking her head. "Must be true love." She nodded towards Alexandria. "Okay, let's go," she said.

"Go where?" Alexandria asked.

"We can't just leave him there. Let's go."

"But our cover…"

"Isn't going to matter one bit if he's dead," Katie replied. "There's light coming from the hallway, so she probably left the door open when she took off. Come on."

"What are we supposed to do?" Alexandria asked with a small edge to her voice.

"Well we can't just leave him there to die," Katie said. "Come on, Alex, seconds count."

"But we…"

"Now!" Katie said more firmly. Without waiting, Katie jumped out of the back of the van and walked quickly toward the entrance to the

Constitution Hotel. Neither woman said a word as they strolled into the hotel lobby and past the Concierge's desk.

"Busy morning?" the concierge said in a friendly tone.

"Beats a dead morning," Katie threw back as they entered the elevator. At the room, the door was slightly ajar. The body was pitched forward, half slumped on the bed with his upper body on the mattress and his lower body on the floor. Katie thought it looked a little like he was praying. He'd better be, she thought to herself.

"Alright, Alex, here's what we're going to do," she said very calmly. "I'm going to pull his head and shoulders back and you're going to take his legs and straighten them out so we can get him flat on the floor on his back." Katie straddled the man's body from around his back and grabbed him under the shoulders and pulled. Alexandria stood nearby, motionless.

"Now would be a good time to help, Alex," Katie said with more than a tad of sarcasm in her voice. "Like right now," she said again as the full weight of the man's body pushed back against her and forced her back into the dresser. Alexandria came forward very reluctantly and with a vile expression, grabbed the man's legs and pulled them. Both women struggled to pull the dead weight of the man around. Katie immediately knelt down beside him and felt for a pulse. When she couldn't find one, she bent her head down to his exposed chest and listened.

"Do you know CPR?" she asked Alexandria as she straddled the man's body and felt for the location of his sternum.

"No… I couldn't," Alexandria answered.

"Come on," Katie said in between thrusts to the man's chest. "Start blowing."

Alexandria's eyes grew wide. "I… I can't."

Katie glanced at her rather sharply. "He's not breathing, Alex, come on. Just lift his chin up, clear his airway, put your mouth on his and blow," Katie said.

Alexandria knelt down very slowly. She brushed away her short, black hair and got close to the man's face.

"Seconds count, Alex."

Alexandria started to bend down toward the man's mouth, but backed away. "I can't," she said quietly.

"You have to," Katie said in between thrusts. "He could suffer brain damage if you don't. Come on, Alex, you can do this."

Again, Alexandria bent forward and got close to the man's mouth and again she immediately sat upright.

"I…I just can't," she said.

Katie shook her head. "If you can't do this, then for God's sakes go find me someone who can."

Alexandria watched for a few seconds as Katie shifted her position, lifted the man's neck with the heel of her hand, and arched his head back. Katie covered the man's mouth with hers and breathed in very slowly, checking to see that his chest was rising.

She looked up for a second. "Damn it, if he has some disease or something, I'll kill him myself," she said.

With that, Alexandria walked out.

After a few minutes of alternating between rescue breathing and compressions, Katie was beginning to wonder how much longer she could last. Her muscles were tiring, her back ached and she felt slightly dizzy and short of breath. After one more set of breaths, she noticed a small rise in the man's chest followed by a slight movement in his arm. She stopped and felt a weak pulse. He at least appeared to be breathing on his own again. She kept a finger on his carotid pulse as the ambulance crew and the Hotel Security officer showed up.

"Cardiac arrest," she told them. "He's been out for approximately six minutes and I've been doing CPR for the last four. Subject's name is Saul Levine and he's probably got ID on him in his wallet."

The EMTs knelt down and relieved Katie of her duties as they started hooking him up to a portable EKG machine.

"Are you related?" one of them asked.

"No."

"Staying with him?"

"No. I was just here to make a delivery," she said as she pulled herself up. Katie quickly grabbed the gift basket before anyone else could ask her any more questions and bolted out the door. She saw Alexandria standing by the elevator with her back turned. Ignoring her completely, Katie pressed the down button. As the elevator doors opened up, she saw two blue uniforms. She quickly jerked her baseball cap way down and held the basket up to obscure her face. The last thing she wanted was to be recognized by one of her former fellow officers and have to explain what she was doing there. Alexandria got on the elevator behind her and they rode down in silence. Neither spoke until Katie got behind the wheel and announced, "I need a drink." Alexandria said nothing.

Katie pulled into her former partner Sean McCleary's bar, the Blue Line.

"Katie, my girl, how are you?" Sean McCleary yelled as he waved to her. Sean's once-red hair was now mostly gray but his eyebrows were still distinctively red and bushy.

"Pissier than thirsty and too thirsty to piss," she answered back sharply. Cocking her thumb back over her shoulder she said, "This is Alexandria."

"A pleasure," Sean said, extending his hand, but Alexandria just stood there.

"She doesn't like to touch or be touched," Katie announced rather loudly, glaring at Alexandria as if to dare her to say anything.

Sean looked curiously at the tall, thin woman and pulled his hand back. "So what can I get for you ladies?" he asked.

"I'll have a Smuttynose Ale," Katie replied.

Sean looked at her curiously. "Have you given up your beloved scotch entirely, Katie?" he asked.

"This is my version of a health food kick," Katie said. "Less alcohol, more water."

"I see," Sean said as he pulled from the tap. "And for you?" he said, nodding toward Alexandria.

"Diet soda, please," Alexandria said quietly. Katie rolled her eyes.

Sean placed their drinks on the bar and Katie grabbed them up and gestured toward a booth. It was early and the Blue Line was nearly empty.

Katie knocked back a good portion of her beer and set the glass down loudly on the table. Alexandria jumped slightly.

"Tell me one thing, Alex," Katie began, "let's say that had been me back there. Let's say I keeled over and wasn't breathing. Would you have helped me?"

"Of course."

"How?" Katie asked.

"I would have gotten you help," Alexandria answered.

"What if I needed CPR? What if I choked right now and needed the Heimlich?"

"Do you need the Heimlich right now?" Alexandria asked.

Katie picked the glass back up and finished off the rest of the beer. Sean looked over but she waved him off.

"I don't understand, Alex," Katie began. "I just don't get it."

"What don't you get?"

"You. This thing. This aversion to being touched." Katie deliberately reached across the table as she said the words and put her hand on Alexandria's arm. Alexandria immediately pulled back.

"He could have died, Alex."

"But he didn't. You saved his life. Your being there made the difference."

"But what if I hadn't been there?" Katie asked. "What if it had been me in trouble? Or Margo? Or Jane? Geez, Jane could go any minute with all those hot flashes she's having. God only knows how screwed up her body is right now. Would you have just stood by and said, 'Sorry, I can't help because I don't like to touch people'?"

"He didn't die, Katie."

"Alex, all I'm saying is that you're missing out on a lot of life because of this…this thing you have. Maybe it's time you talked to someone about it. Maybe someone could help you work through this and figure out the reason."

"What makes you think I don't know the reason?"

ABOUT THE AUTHOR

Felicia Donovan is a recognized expert in the field of law enforcement technology, and currently works at a New England-based police department as a civilian Information Systems manager. She swears by the adage, "every keystroke is recoverable," and has worked on the forensic recovery of files and data from computers used in crimes. She is also renowned for her ability to digitally enhance photographs and has assisted the FBI on cases related to digital photography, as well as providing technical advice relative to cyber crimes.

She is the founder of CLEAT (Communication, Law Enforcement and Technology), an organization comprised of law enforcement professionals around the New England region, and is a member of the International Association of Chiefs of Police and the New Hampshire Police Association.

Donovan lives in New Hampshire with her two children who don't shed, and three dogs that do.